The Vinegar Peak Wars

Saddle tramps Cephas Dannehar and Slim Oskin drifted into the Vinegar Peak country of Arizona Territory, helped an old colleague out of trouble, were taken for hired gunmen and bucked the interest of the Black Eagle copper mine and scheming Nate Sturgis, the self-styled Boss of Vinegar Peak.

In a lead-peppered struggle between their horse-ranching friends and Sturgis's toughs, known as the Peace Commission, bullets were soon flying and fires of destruction were lit. All part of the growing pains of a raw western territory, molding its post-Civil War destiny.

Dannehar and Oskin were no angels but, throwing their guns in on the side of right, they faced a war which could see Vinegar Peak become respectable or its violent citizenry, prodded by grasping ambitions, might make it an outlaw town ruled by thuggery and the lawless gun.

The Vinegar Peak Wars

Hugh Martin

A Black Horse Western

ROBERT HALE · LONDON

© A. A. Glynn 2011
First published in Great Britain 2012

ISBN 978-0-7090-9369-5

Robert Hale Limited
Clerkenwell House
Clerkenwell Green
London EC1R 0HT

www.halebooks.com

Typeset by
Derek Doyle & Associates, Shaw Heath
Printed and bound in Great Britain by
CPI Antony Rowe, Chippenham and Eastbourne

CHAPTER ONE

THE HARD LUCK POSSE

The five riders came down the desert trail at a slow pace, raising plumes of dust touched by the blazing Arizona sun rising towards its mid-day intensity. There were two to the front and two to the rear with Bert Flinders in the middle, riding with his hands tied behind his back.

His captors were plainly hard cases, all in range gear. Saddle tramps Cephas Dannehar and Slim Oskin, riding up the trail from the opposite direction, squinted against the glare of the sun to take in the scene. As they drew nearer, Oskin gasped: 'That's Flinders they have trussed up there! It's Bert Flinders for sure!'

'It is,' said Cephas Dannehar. 'It is and no mistake!'

There had been Indian trouble in New Mexico that year of 1876 and former Confederate Dannehar and ex-Union trooper Oskin had completed a spell as scouts for the army contingent at Fort Truelove and were now riding towards whatever they found awaiting them over the next horizon. They had not bargained for the startling sight of their former scouting colleague, Bert Flinders, tied up and under the escort of four riders – none of whom sported the star of a lawman.

The pair, both in their early thirties, continued to allow their horses to walk slowly towards the party, keeping their eyes fixed on the escort and with their right hands dropped towards the butts of their six-guns.

'I don't like the look of this,' murmured Dannehar.

'Nor do I,' said Oskin. 'The jaspers who're holding him have no badges of office and, anyway, I'd say if there was ever man unlikely to be a lawbreaker it's Bert Flinders.'

'Looks like they're headed for the same place we are, to water their horses,' commented Dannehar nodding in the direction of the sparse splash of greenery that indicated a waterhole in the garish desert landscape. 'Let's go right ahead and meet up with them, but take care – that's a particularly ugly joker up front.'

The bigger of the pair of leading riders was a paunchy, bearded individual who seemed to have the demeanour of a leader. Plainly, the escort had noted the coming of Dannehar and Oskin but, instead of riding ahead to meet the pair, they followed the big man who jerked his head toward the waterhole then veered off in that direction. Oskin and Dannehar also swung their mounts towards the oasis and plodded onward, still keeping alert.

'Don't let on that we know Flinders,' breathed Dannehar.

'D'you figure we can spring him loose?' queried Oskin.

'We can try.'

Oskin and Dannehar and the four riders and prisoner met at the water-hole, which proved to be a grass fringed sink, fed by a spring.

Instead of attending immediately to watering their horses, the escort and prisoner waited for Dannehar and Oskin to catch up with them. There was the suggestion of trouble in the offing in the way the four sat scowling in their saddles.

The big bearded man had hard black eyes, shaded by a broad sombrero, and he and his three companions had the look of cow wranglers who had turned their talents to something other than the cowboy trade. All wore Colt or Smith & Wesson revolvers at their belts. Bert Flinders, darkly handsome and in his mid-thirties, sat in their midst with defiance on his face. He showed no sign of recognizing Dannehar and Oskin.

Nevertheless, Dannehar greeted his escort, saying: 'Howdy. Looks like you've got yourselves a real bad customer there, whoever he might be,' hoping to convey to Flinders the need to refrain from showing recognition.

'Sure,' said the big man in a grating voice. 'He's a bad one, all right.'

'You fellows peace officers?' asked Slim Oskin with something like wide eyed innocence.

'We're part of the Peace Commission of Vinegar Peak,' said the big man as he swung out of his saddle and took the reins of his horse, leading it to the water.

His companions followed his example, one of them taking the bridle of Flinders's horse and leading it along with his own, with the bound Flinders still in his saddle.

At the mention of a Vinegar Peak's Peace Commission, Dannehar and Oskin simultaneously felt suspicious. In their experience, the so-called peace commissions of cowtowns and booming mining camps were invariably covers, enabling gangs of unscrupulous leading citizens to keep the control of the gambling dens and joy houses in their own hands. The pair had passed through the unimpressive little town of Vinegar Peak a couple of hours before.

All four of the Peace Commission riders stood with their horses and that of Flinders at the water with their backs to the still mounted Dannehar and Oskin while the animals drank. Dannehar winked at Oskin and indicated his own Winchester carbine in its saddle scabbard then slid it out of its housing noiselessly. Slim Oskin got the message and did the same.

Each pumped his carbine in unison and the sound caused the men at the water to whirl around abruptly.

'What the hell—?' grated the big man at the sight of the two saddle tramps, alert and keen eyed and coolly holding their carbines levelled unwaveringly towards them.

'Hoist your hands!' commanded Dannehar. 'Keep them up, well away from your guns.'

Scowling, the four from Vinegar Peak obeyed but the big man spluttered a protest. 'What the hell are you trying to do? We're taking a man in for bank robbery.'

Oskin grinned. 'Peace commissions don't stack up to having much legitimacy in our view, mister,' he said.

Bert Flinders, in his saddle, had turned his head around to Dannehar and Oskin and looked as surprised as his escort.

'Drop your hands to your belt buckles and

loosen your shell belts then drop them and your guns to the ground,' commanded Dannehar. 'We'll let daylight into anyone trying to go for his gun. Do it now and then put your hands up again.'

The sullen faced Vinegar Peak men dropped their belts with holstered six-guns attached to the ground and lifted their arms again.

Dannehar kept his carbine levelled at the Peace Commission men while Oskin came down from his saddle, walked the few paces to Flinders's horse with his Winchester held in the crook of his arm while, with his free hand, he took his Bowie knife from his belt. He quickly cut the rope binding Flinders's hands behind his back. Flinders rubbed his chafed hands gratefully.

'Thanks, Slim,' he breathed with a relieved grin, 'I sure didn't expect you two to show up. I figured my goose was cooked.'

Oskin, noticing that Flinders was weaponless, stooped, quickly picked up one of the grounded shellbelts and its holstered Colt and handed them to him.

'That'll adjust the odds,' he said. 'I guess these gents deprived you of your gun so exchange is no robbery.'

Flinders buckled on the belt, then levelled his newly acquired weapon at the group of dismounted Vinegar Peak men already covered by Dannehar's Winchester. Dannehar, still keeping the men covered, urged his mount forward to allow it to drink while Oskin led his own horse to the water by the bridle.

'You won't get away with this,' growled the leader of the posse. Dannehar paid no attention to this protest but gestured with his carbine towards the horses of the Vinegar Peak men. 'Step over to your horses and unsaddle them,' he ordered. 'Put your saddles on the ground. Anyone attempting to go for the gun in his saddle scabbard will be dosed with hot lead.'

The four men stepped reluctantly towards their horses, unfastened their saddle cinches and lifted their saddles down to the ground. Slim Oskin, with his horse refreshed, climbed back into his saddle and continued to keep his Winchester trained on the men from Vinegar Peak.

'Now, haze your cayuses off,' commanded Dannehar.

'What?' howled the men in unison.

'Haze 'em off, away from the water! C'mon, jump to it! Slap 'em and holler at 'em!' urged Dannehar.

The four men began to do so in a half-hearted fashion which caused Dannehar to give a full blooded Confederate rebel yell so that the horses pranced.

'Slap 'em!' he commanded and the Vinegar Peak men slapped the rumps of their animals with

11

little enthusiasm. Slim Oskin contributed a blood curdling screech and the four unburdened horses jerked nervously then ran off into the desert in panic.

'Hell, you can't do this to us,' wailed one man.

'We're doing it whether you like it or not,' grinned Oskin.

'You can't leave us out here on the desert without horses,' hooted the big, bearded man. 'It's nothing but plain murder.'

'Quit squawking,' growled Dannehar. 'You know damned well they'll naturally drift back to the water in no time. You'll just have to hang around here for a while until they do.'

The Vinegar Peak men stood in glowering rage with their guns, shellbelts and saddles at their feet while the dwindling plumes of hoof stirred dust out on the desert marked the disappearance of their horses.

Dannehar, Oskin and Flinders backed their horses away from the group of Peace Commission men, still keeping their firearms levelled, then they turned swiftly and hit a smart lick for the desert on drumming hoofs.

The bearded man shook his fist and bellowed after them: 'We'll make you pay for this. By thunder, we'll sure as hell make you pay!'

CHAPTER TWO

TROUBLE AT VINEGAR PEAK

'So, did you rob a bank?' asked Slim Oskin.

'Yeah, when we parted company at Fort Truelove, you said you were coming to Arizona to help your brother run his horse ranch,' put in Cephas Dannehar. 'Then we find you trussed up by a posse, seeming to have turned criminal. What's your story?'

It was mid-afternoon and the three, having made a fast dash over the desert, were taking a break at another waterhole, slaking their thirst, watering their horses and replenishing their canteens. They took some gleeful satisfaction from thinking of the plight of the men from Vinegar

Peak whose horses would automatically drift back to the water but, by the time they were saddled, Dannehar, Oskin and Flinders would have had such a good start that pursuit would be futile. Even at that moment, the four might be making their disconsolate way back to Vinegar Peak.

'You fellows know me well enough to know I'd never rob a bank,' Flinders said. 'I walked right into a trap. It's an ugly story and the polecats who'd have you believe they're the outstanding, honest citizens of Vinegar Peak and pillars of the community are at the back of it.

'I came back to my brother's place. It's a few miles the other side of Vinegar Peak and good land considering it's desert-edge rangeland. My brother, Will, was making out fairly well but just before I showed up after scouting for the army, he began to be harassed by a bunch of businessmen; the so called respectable citizens who make up the Peace Commission.'

'We came through Vinegar Peak and it didn't look as if it supported much in the way of business,' commented Oskin.

'Oh, don't be fooled,' said Flinders. 'It's prosperous enough and it has big ambitions for itself. The business faction figures it can build itself up into a place of importance in the Territory. The Black Eagle copper mine is a mainstay of the place and its big boss, Nate Sturgis, controls the Peace

14

Commission. The whole Peace Commission wants the town connected to the railroad, which would suit the Black Eagle bosses just fine. At present, they ship out their ore by horse and wagon but they have plans to create a big operation with sheds and loading bays right beside the rails. The trouble is, they claim the best place for the rails and their big operation is right on our land. They tried to tempt Will with offers to buy his W-Bar-F outfit that were plumb insulting.'

Cephas Dannehar took a swig from his canteen. 'So is your brother holding out for a better price?' he asked.

'Not on your life,' said Flinders. 'He worked hard to build up a good little outfit and he's breeding good horseflesh, helped out by four reliable hands. He told the Peace Commission and the Black Eagle gang to go to hell. Will's a determined type but quieter than me. I'm backing him all the way.

'I got into his feud with the vested interests in Vinegar Peak. I admit I'm kind of mouthy and I made it plain that the W-Bar-F would sooner fight than take their measly offers.'

Oskin grinned. 'That sounds like the Bert Flinders we know so well. You always were stubborn and a hell of a fellow to stand his ground. That's what made you a good army scout.'

'Well, this time, I got myself into the hole you

15

just pulled me out of,' Flinders admitted. 'The Peace Commission and the mine owners don't like people who stand up to them. In fact, that bunch of progressive citizens amount to what's almost an outlaw gang and it has a crew of riders to do its pushing. You recently had the dubious pleasure of meeting some of them. Pretty soon, they were uttering threats against Will and me and I found it damned hard to keep my temper. I even got into a fist fight with one of their hard cases in a saloon a couple of weeks back – that didn't go down well with the Peace Commission and its friends.'

As the sun began to descend and the three continued to take their ease beside the waterhole, Bert Flinders unfolded more of his tale.

He told how he and his brother continued in their defiance and the tempers of their opponents grew ever more ugly. Then, on the evening before Dannehar and Oskin rescued him, he rode into town intending to make some purchases and have a drink but he never reached the store or the saloon.

With the town in semi-darkness, he was leading his horse to a hitching rack when a group of men rushed out of an alley, overpowered him and hit him over the head to render him unconscious before he could put up a fight.

He just had time to recognize them as some of the squad of riders maintained by the Peace

Commission, led by burly, heavily bearded Bull Tuke.

When he came round, he found he was trussed up and tied to his horse in the middle of a mounted group commanded by Tuke and they were traversing the desert.

'You sure are about to get your come-uppance, Flinders,' hooted Tuke on seeing that he was conscious. 'When Judge Palmer comes in on circuit, he'll take a strong line when he hears how we saw you coming out of the bank after you broke in when it was closed. He'll send you to the penitentiary for sure. You figured you'd made a right smart escape, bolting for the desert the way you did but, by thunder, we came right after you. Too bad you came away empty handed. It shows how all-fired stupid you are that you didn't realize all the money would be locked in the safe for the night.'

Now Flinders saw the whole plot which certainly had the hand of the Vinegar Peak Peace Commission behind it. Tuke and his companions put an elaborate scheme into action having knocked him senseless. They had taken him out on to the desert to give the impression that he had tried to escape and they planned to ride back to Vinegar Peak in triumph, boasting and lying that they had gallantly pursued him in a chase over the wilderness after witnessing his fictitious break-in at the closed-up bank. Gullible citizens with their money in the bank would be sure to fall for the yarn and readily turn against him.

'They had the whole thing neatly planned,' said Flinders. 'I figured they busted the door of the bank to make it look as if someone had broken in. Judge Palmer is a slippery old snake, rumoured to be corrupt and in the pocket of the Peace Commission. I'd get damned little justice and be jailed for a long stretch.'

Cephas Dannehar gave a low whistle. 'Looks like the Peace Commission is real bad medicine if it plans that kind of crooked move.'

'It's as I told you. With that outfit ruling the roost in Vinegar Peak, the place is damned near an outlaw town,' said Flinders.

'Isn't there any regular peace officer in Vinegar Peak?' asked Dannehar.

'There's old Marshal Tom Cope, but he's wholly the Peace Commission's man. There's something plumb disturbing in the wind. Bull Tuke and his crew didn't go to all the trouble of trapping me just for fun. It was all part of something bigger or I miss my guess, and it can only be connected with the Black Eagle's greed for the W-Bar-F land.'

'Sounds like trouble just over the hill,' murmured Slim Oskin giving an involuntary nudge to his holstered six-gun.

'Sure does,' agreed Dannehar. 'Some kind of

action will be healthy for you, Slim. I've noticed that your recent idle life is almost making you fat.'

'You mean you fellows are throwing in with Will and me?' asked Bert Flinders.

'Well, it looks like you and your brother are a worthy cause that should be supported,' said Dannehar lazily.

'And since we are doing nothing but drifting, we might as well take a hand in the game. Having met that ugly *hombre*, Tuke, and his sidekicks, I'd sure like to take another swipe at them,' declared Oskin. 'So what's our next move?'

'To head for the W-Bar-F. It lies on the other side of Vinegar Peak,' Flinders said. 'We can circle the town. I reckon it would be dangerous for me to show up there if Tuke and his crew manage to get there first. The whole damned Peace Commission will be out for my blood.'

They decided to travel in the cool of the evening, rested their horses further, ate some of the beef jerky Dannehar and Oskin carried and saddled up as the desert sun descended on the horizon. Dannehar and Oskin felt an invigorating rising of their spirits at the prospect of some action after their wearying horseback miles.

The trio made good progress without forcing their horses and, with night fully enfolding the land, they reached the beginnings of the desert edge pastures. The landscape of cactus and sun-

19

split rocks gradually changed, becoming lush and freshly scented. When the moon slipped out from scudding clouds, it gave the wide vistas of the terrain a silvered beauty.

They circled Vinegar Peak, whose scattered yellow lit windows they saw lying below them. A further half hour of riding brought them within sight of the darkened structures of the W-Bar-F ranch. As they neared it, the moonlight picked out a long, low house backed by barns, stables and corrals in which several heads of horses were penned.

Flinders led the way into the ranch yard and hailed the house. The front door opened, sending a shaft of light across the gallery and into it stepped a tall man who – even at a distance – had a marked resemblance to Bert Flinders, though he sported a longhorn moustache and was obviously older.

'Bert!' he called. 'Where the Sam Hill have you been?'

'Tangling with Bull Tuke and the Peace Commission's roughnecks,' responded Bert Flinders. 'I brought a couple of old friends to meet you and all three of us are in need of some nourishing grub.'

The three swung off their mounts and Will Flinders called to two of his hands who, alerted by the sound of the arriving horses, had drifted into the yard from the bunkhouse. 'Bob, Pedro, unsaddle these cayuses and give them water and feed and tell Walt to rustle up some substantial grub for these three boys.'

Dannehar, Oskin and Bert Flinders mounted the gallery and entered the comfortably equipped living room of the ranch house. Bert Flinders introduced Dannehar and Oskin as two who were throwing in their lot with the brothers and the trio settled gratefully into easy chairs.

Bert Flinders gave his brother a detailed account of his exploits since leaving the house the previous evening and of his rescue by Dannehar and Oskin. Walt Harris, a hand who counted cooking among his gifts, came in with a tray laden with meat, potatoes, vegetables and coffee to which the three began to do immediate justice.

Hearing his brother's tale, Will Flinders shook his head. 'This tale about you breaking into the bank after it closed is the damnedest, most far-fetched thing I ever heard,' he exclaimed, 'but I reckon there are people in town who'll fall for it. The whole move by the Peace Commission – grabbing you, taking you out on the desert to make a show of capturing you, claiming you ran for it – sure shows that they're turning ugly. It makes me wonder what they'll do next and they're sure to come up with some dirty trick.'

'More likely a whole bag of 'em,' said Bert Flinders. 'I wonder if they'll push the bank robbery trick. Maybe they'll try to get their hands on me again.'

'And on Slim and me into the bargain.' said Cephas Dannehar. 'After all, we busted you loose from what they claimed was the custody of a citizen's arrest.'

Will Flinders frowned. 'They sure as shooting will not let things lie as they are. That black whiskered skunk, Nate Sturgis, the boss of the Black Eagle mine, controls the Peace Commission and the whole crew of 'em are out to grab our land. When it comes to numbers, the odds are against us.'

'Speaking of shooting,' said his brother, 'we have very little ammunition on the place and this whole mess could come to shooting before we know it. I'll take the buckboard into town tomorrow and collect ammunition from Andy Bright's store.'

'No,' said Will Flinders sharply. 'You're sure to run into trouble. The town will be alerted to that fool robbery story and you could get Tom Cope and the Peace Commission on your neck. You better lie low here. And there's another thing – with the Peace Commission intensifying opposition to us, they could have put out word around town that we're not to be served by the storekeepers.'

'Slim and I could do that chore,' suggested

Dannehar. 'After all, we're strangers in town. No one will connect us to the W-Bar-F.'

'That's a sound idea,' agreed the elder brother. 'Take saddle panniers to carry the ammunition instead of the buckboard, it'll be too easily recognized as our property. The boys will fix you some sleeping accommodation in the bunkhouse and you can start out after breakfast.'

Oskin and Dannehar were introduced to the W-Bar-F crew: Bob Trickett, the foreman; Walt Harris, Pedro Ruiz and Harry Scott, the oldest man on the ranch, and reputedly one of the best horse wranglers in the southwest. After their most comfortable night's sleep for weeks, they were served with one of Walt Harris's best breakfasts and prepared to ride into Vinegar Peak. They were armed with a list of the ammunition required and instructions as to the trails to take into the town.

They reached Vinegar Peak just as the sun was reaching its full strength and rode into a dusty single street, lined with sun warped timber buildings which had the impermanent look of a boom town's sructures. On a hill on the further side of town stark against the wide sky, stood the rig of the Black Eagle mine, marking the copper strike that brought the settlement into being.

The gun dealer's store was a clapboard building with the name of Andrew Bright emblazoned over its window. Dannehar and Oskin drew rein outside it, swung down from their saddles, entered and found Andy Bright to be a thin, middle aged man, standing behind a counter backed by a selection of firearms and boxes of ammunition. He looked with deep suspicion at the pair of strangers doubtless affected by their saddle tramp appearance and their low slung holsters. Such a pair might be owlhoot outlaws on the dodge.

He nodded a greeting and his suspicion found its way into his voice when he said: 'Good morning, gents. I haven't the pleasure of your acquaintance.'

'That's right. You haven't,' said Slim Oskin. 'We're travelling men and we only recently arrived in your fair town.'

'And we require some ammunition,' Dannehar said, laying the list of requirements on the counter.

Bright picked up the list and looked at it. 'Cartridges for Colt revolvers, Winchesters and Henry rifles and a tolerable long list,' he commented, still with a hint of suspicion.

Cephas Dannehar fixed him with a stony gaze. 'Being travelling men, we go well prepared. We've tangled with hostile Apaches in the past and might easily do so in the future,' he stated. 'And we're backing the order with sound dollars.'

From his shirt pocket, he produced part of the wad of bills provided by the Flinders brothers.

Andy Bright turned and began to select boxes of

24

ammunition from the shelves and place them on the counter, the prospect of profit having obviously quelled his suspicions of the pair of strangers who seemed to be equipping a small army.

Dannehar and Oskin checked the purchases, Dannehar handed over the payment and the two left the store with their arms full of cartridge boxes.

They had just finished packing the boxes into their saddle panniers when they heard a harsh hoot from across the street.

'Well, look at who we have here! It's the two trail tramps who're so good at rescuing thieving polecats like Bert Flinders from lawful arrest!'

Coming across the street were six men. In the lead was a white moustached old timer with a lawman's star on his shirt, obviously Marshal Tom Cope. Beside him strode the hulking, bearded Bull Tuke. Others in the group were recognizable as some of the Peace Commission riders from whom Flinders had been snatched.

Tuke's mouth was drawn back in a broken toothed grin. Plainly emboldened by being backed by a superior number, he led his companions directly towards Dannehar and Oskin, swinging a pair of huge balled fists.

'We've got this pair where we want them, boys,' he snarled. 'Now the boot's on the other foot!'

CHAPTER THREE

UGLY RUMBLINGS

Standing by their tethered horses, Dannehar and Oskin stiffened into belligerent poses as the six men strode towards them with Bull Tuke quickening his pace to put himself into the lead. He came almost within reach of Dannehar who was watching Tuke's right hand, anticipating any move towards his holster.

'I said we'd get even with you grubby drifters and, by God, we're going to enjoy putting you in your place,' Tuke growled.

He thrust his hand towards his gun butt and was almost face to face with Dannehar – a move which suggested he was about to gut shoot him, putting a bullet in his innards from close range. The move was his big mistake, for Dannehar simply grabbed his ample beard and hauled him forward, causing Tuke to bellow with pain and rage and flail his arms.

Dannehar lifted his right leg, planted his boot in Tuke's belly, released his beard and, with his foot, shoved the big man backward. He scooted on his boot heels, and teetered off balance into the midst of his companions, two of whom were knocked off their feet. Tuke joined them, falling heavily into the dust of the street.

Within the same split second, Oskin had reacted to Tuke's grab for his gun, drawing his Colt with a lightning fast action. He jumped forward and, even as Tuke and two of his companions were sent sprawling, he brought the barrel of his weapon down on the hat of the nearest man to him, knocking him senseless.

Marshal Tom Cope showed astonishing sprightliness for an old man – diving to one side, mounting the plankwalk and taking refuge behind a packing case standing outside the establishment next to the gun store. He peered, white faced, over the top of the case and, to nobody in particular, shouted hoarsely: 'No shooting! There's a town ordinance against shooting on the street!'

So far as the last of Tuke's companions still left standing was concerned, he could have saved his breath because he showed no inclination towards gunplay. He was standing stock still, staring at

Dannehar and Oskin both of whom were now lev-elling six-guns.

Dannehar grinned at the scene in front of the gun store. Bull Tuke, badly winded, still sprawled in the rutted and hoof-pocked dust; the two with whom he collided were picking themselves up without any show of fight; another lay senseless and one was standing frozen as though hypnotised and Vinegar Peak's officer of the law had sought a place of safety.

'Seems to me we had you Peace Commission men in a similar position just a few hours ago,' taunted Dannehar. 'You sure are sticklers for pun-ishment. We aim to ride out, leaving you embarrassed yet again. Pay heed to the marshal and don't try any shooting as we go because we'll shoot back, ordinance or no ordinance. And you wouldn't want to test our trigger savvy.'

Each using one hand, the pair unhitched their horses, quickly holstered their weapons, mounted and spurred the animals. They leapt forward in a stirring of dust, with Dannehar and Oskin bending low over their saddle horns.

'You sure didn't earn Tuke's affection by nearly pulling his whiskers from his chin,' shouted Oskin over the beating hoofs.

'I reckon not,' called Dannehar. Behind them, someone broke the town's ordinance and defied Dannehar's warning by loosing a pistol shot that sent a slug whining close to Dannehar's ear. 'And I figure that's Tuke, expressing his disaffection!' added Dannehar. 'Let's get the hell out of this bit of scenery before the whole bunch of 'em gather their wits and come after us!'

With the heavily laden panniers of ammunition slapping their horses' flanks, the two pounded the trail back to the W-Bar-F without any pursuit from the town and came at length into the ranch yard on lathered and steaming animals. The Flinders brothers and three of the hands were in the yard and they noted the heavy appearance of the panniers.

'You got the ammunition!' exclaimed Bert Flinders.

'Sure thing, and we stirred up the hornet's nest some more,' said Oskin. 'Cephas nearly removed Tuke's chin whiskers.'

'Without the benefit of a razor,' added Dannehar.

The W-Bar-F men hooted with laughter when Oskin gave a dramatic account of Dannehar's yanking of Bull Tuke's beard but the certainty of drastic repercussions of Dannehar and Oskin's venture into Vinegar Peak did not escape them.

'The Peace Commission gang know well enough that you are connected with us after your first run-in with them and now they know we're stacking up ammunition,' Will Flinders said.

'Maybe it was too much to hope they could go into town without being spotted,' said his brother. 'Still, I figure there's every chance Andy Bright would put word around that two strangers bought ammunition from him even if Tuke and his friends hadn't seen you. He might claim to be independent but you can bet he's as much in cahoots with the Peace Commission as most of the storekeepers.'

'I guess grabbing Tuke by the beard was the same as grabbing a tiger by the tail,' said Dannehar. 'I suppose there'll be repercussions.'

'No doubt there's a ruckus in the wind, but we'll make good and sure we're ready for it,' Will Flinders said.

Back in Vinegar Peak, the repercussions were set in motion that very afternoon with the calling of what was grandly termed a 'town meeting' in the settlement's court room. Storekeepers, tradesmen, saloonkeepers and dance hall proprietors and a fair number of Black Eagle miners crammed into the premises. Nate Sturgis, the self appointed chairman, stood before the crowd on a dais that gave added stature to his already large figure.

Nate Sturgis was accustomed to having his own way and to using a heavy hand to get it. He was president of the Black Eagle Mining Company which made him virtual boss of Vinegar Peak. He had a coarse, lined face, fringed by black mutton chop whiskers and his prosperous appearance in a broadcloth suit, with a showy watch chain across its well filled vest did little to cover the manners and personality of a man who had started out as a two-fisted, hard scrabble miner in the boom towns of the western territories.

Cunning, double dealing and ruthlessness had brought him to the top position on the company's board and he was ever ready to employ all three to push Black Eagle's fortunes yet further. The Vinegar Peak Peace Commission was a tool of Black Eagle's command of the town and it was wholly the instrument of Nate Sturgis.

Other frontier settlements had their peace commissions, which were usually a set of owners of the big gambling houses and saloons and merely fronts for protection schemes. They ensured that a good percentage of the profits made by lesser saloons, gambling dens and the controllers of the painted ladies, delicately called 'soiled doves', flowed into the hands of the commission's controllers.

Such commissions had their squads of enforcers but Nate Sturgis had improved upon their methods. He had canvassed the storekeepers and tradesmen of Vinegar Peak and enlisted them in the Peace Commission, giving it the appearance of a respectable civic body. Then, telling them that the copper strike on which the town was built was so valuable, ensuring their own prosperity, that it made Vinegar Peak a prime target for lawless predators, he built up his squad of hard cases led by Bull Tuke. To the town's commercial establishment, they were defenders of the citizenry. To Nate Sturgis, they were his miniature private army.

His harsh, indignant voice pierced the pall of tobacco smoke hanging over the gathering as he gave an account of what he would have the citizenry believe were grave threats to the wellbeing of Vinegar Peak.

'Fellow citizens,' he thundered, 'it's time to alert you to the dangers that are lurking in the vicinity of our town; dangers that threaten our peace, prosperity and our future as a progressive community, solidly based on sound business.

'You all know the Flinders brothers who run the W-Bar-F horse ranch and you know how, in the interests of sound business and putting this town on the map by way of a railroad link, they have been made several handsome offers for their land. Any reasonable rancher would have accepted but Will and Bert Flinders turned down the offers point-blank, setting themselves up as enemies of progress and prosperity. And Bert Flinders has made himself objectionable with his aggressive attitude.

'That's bad enough but there is worse news. Bert Flinders has shown himself to be a sneaking thief.

Not that he actually stole anything but he had that intention and what he aimed to steal was the hard earned cash that you solid citizens deposited in the bank.' Sturgis paused while a collective angry growl rumbled through the crowd.

'I'm glad to say that his evil intentions were foiled by the stout hearted men retained by the Peace Commission to keep our town safe,' he continued. 'Bert Flinders wasn't man enough to take any chances. It's a sad fact that there are men who rob banks by stepping inside in the light of day and holding up the tellers with firearms. Reprehensible though that is, at least the robbers take chances and frequently lose their lives. Flinders was having none of that. No, fellow citizens, he waited until night when the bank was closed and he broke in by forcing a door.'

At the back of the room, some of the group standing with Bull Tuke smirked among themselves, remembering that it was they who, after knocking Bert Flinders unconscious, forced the door of the bank to provide evidence of a break in.

Nate Sturgis grew yet more dramatic in his narrative. 'Now, I guess it goes to show how plumb stupid Flinders was that he did not reckon on all the money in the bank being in the safe for the night.

'He could not break into the safe and there was not even one red cent of petty cash to be found in the drawers. He sneaked out of the bank the way he came in, a frustrated man. But he was spotted, fellow citizens, spotted by the vigilant Peace Commission riders who are ever ready to serve you. True, he managed to mount his horse and ride hard for the desert when he realized that his game was up. Oh, he gave them a good chase and eluded his pursuers for some time, that can't be denied, but he was caught several miles out of town.'

Sturgis dropped his voice to a heavy rumble. 'Then, fellow citizens, something very grave happened. Two gunslingers – exactly the kind of men this town has attempted to keep out – busted on to the scene and, working with the connivance of Flinders himself, managed to break him free in spite of the brave attempts of his captors to hold him. The methods they used were nothing short of murderous. In fact, they attempted to leave a body of men out in the wilderness without horses.'

There was some embarrassed shuffling of feet among Tuke's hard cases at the back of the room, as the memory of their humiliation by Dannehar and Oskin was revived, and Sturgis skated over that part of his narration quickly. In truth, he was furious about the way Dannehar and Oskin had outwitted the Peace Commission's strongarm men on two occasions and, while he had bellowed his displeasure at them in private, in this public arena, he attempted to portray them as heroes. He raised his voice and declared thunderously: 'Two gun-slingers, note, fellow citizens, the sort of lawless outcasts who are holding back civilised progress here in Arizona Territory. Flinders scooted back to the W-Bar-F and those two gunmen came into town this very morning and brazenly secured a fair quantity of ammunition from Andy Bright's store.

'I don't blame Mr Bright for serving them. Like every man here, he's a peaceful citizen and what peaceful man who values his skin dare refuse to deal with a couple of gun carrying ruffians who enter his store and intimidate him?'

Sturgis hoped he could disguise the uncomfort-able incident that followed Dannehar and Oskin's purchase of the ammunition but Wally Drever, the town's blacksmith, a man of noted cantankerous temperament, interrupted: 'How about that ruckus on the street this morning? I saw it from my shop. I didn't see it start but I saw Bull Tuke and others sprawling on the street and two strangers pointing their guns while they mounted their horses – and Town Marshal Cope, yonder, was hiding behind a packing case.'

Old Marshal Tom Cope, standing on the edge of the gathering, tried to make himself as small as possible and the citizenry made a disgruntled rum-bling.

'I'd say,' persisted Drever, 'that the Peace

35

Commission's men outnumbered the two strangers. They didn't give much of an account of themselves.'

It was not often that Nate Sturgis was heckled in public, but brawny Wally Drever was not a man to be cowed, even by the boss of Vinegar Peak.

Sturgis turned a shade of purple; his black whiskers bristled angrily and in near desperation, he lied lamely: 'The Peace Commission's riders almost captured those two this morning but they refrained from any shooting on the street; there's an ordinance against it, remember. And those two gunslingers meant business and might well have shot up the whole town. They're a pair of hired gunfighters, brought in by Will and Bert Flinders who are now showing their hand. They aim to fight, resisting any attempt to buy their land. That's the reason those two showed up here and the reason for their large purchase of ammunition.'

Wally Drever grunted and, under his breath, muttered: 'And they hornswoggled Bull Tuke's crew while Tom Cope hid himself. Some guardians of law and order!'

Sturgis raised his voice yet louder, trying to quell any further heckling. He had called this meeting to spearhead opposition to the Flinders brothers. He wanted drastic action against them and his oratory now became rabble rousing hectoring.

36

'A large purchase of ammunition!' he repeated loudly. 'And a pair of dangerous gunslingers brought in from outside. Why, one of them even made the boast on the street that they couldn't be matched for gun savvy. That's the kind of men they are. That's an indication of what Will and Bert Flinders aim to bring to this country – an out and out war, like the wars between the cattlemen and the settlers. Once it starts, it'll spread, with more drifting gunslingers coming in, looking for wages, or simply because they enjoy killing. I fear for the whole population of our town if things should ever come to such a pass. I say we stop the Flinders and their hired gunsharps right now before they get a chance to use one bullet against us – because that's who they are making war against – us, the people of Vinegar Peak who want to see the prosperity a link to the railroad will bring. We have every right to mount an attack on the W-Bar-F. Firstly, Bert Flinders, a sneaking bank burglar who should be arrested, is hiding out there and, secondly and more important, the Flinders brothers are plotting armed villainy with the help of two dangerous men who're probably on the owlhoot trail and wanted elsewhere. I say we take immediate action!'

Despite the dissenting voice of Wally Drever, Nate Sturgis was beginning to have an effect on the meeting with his predictions of bloody times to come.

Bert Flinders had called Vinegar Peak almost an outlaw town and he knew there was an ugly streak under its surface that was now beginning to manifest itself.

As well as the body of tough miners employed by the Black Eagle company, most of those who earned a living as merchants or tradesmen came into the town on the heels of the copper strike. So long as the mine produced its ore, they were assured of prosperity and they regarded the mine as their milch cow. Almost every one of them supported the plan dreamed up by Nate Sturgis which would bring rails, yards and loading facilities for ore on the land currently occupied by Will Flinders's horse ranch. It would mean further prosperity for the mine and so the town's businessmen would flourish further.

In its way, the fact that the company of riders that was almost the private army of Nate Sturgis could function as the supposed guardians of law and order was a symptom of Vinegar Peak's collective jealous husbandry of the copper resource. Bull Tuke's set of hard cases could be relied on to keep outsiders at bay and, in the past had driven some people out of the insular town.

The ugly turn of mind that lay just under the surface of Vinegar Peak was played upon by Nate Sturgis and his hooting oratory conjured up a vision of the Flinders brothers forced off the

W-Bar-F and the mine's prosperity advanced by its occupation of the ranch's land.

His demand for immediate action brought a hoarse shout from the body of the hall: 'That's right, Mr Sturgis – immediate action! That's the American way of doing things! The way of the old Minute Men, always ready to fight a threat to the citizens!'

The fact that the vociferous enthusiast was Hank Tasker, the town drunk, was overlooked. Vinegar Peak's ugly streak was rising to the surface.

There was a collective growling and another voice yelled: 'That's right! Let's settle the hash of the Flinders and their pair of gunslingers right now! *Right now!*'

CHAPTER FOUR

THE RAID

The body of horsemen crested a rise some distance from the W-Bar-F and came slowly down into the basin which enfolded the ranch's buildings and pastures. It was past midnight and the fugitive moon touched highlights to the carbines and revolvers carried nakedly by the riders now that they were within striking distance of their objective.

Ring bits were muffled to prevent their jingling and every man in the column rode in strict silence, following the orders of Nate Sturgis who was in the lead with nondescript range gear substituted for his respectable broadcloth.

The rabble rousing of the boss of Vinegar Peak had produced the effect he desired and the savage frontier spirit lying just under the town's surface had been stirred to grip the passions of the more easily swayed, many of whom considered themselves to be model citizens.

Mingled with the Peace Commission's riders and led by a vengeance hungry Bull Tuke and a squad of Black Eagle miners who welcomed the chance of a fight as a break from toiling for ore, they were mounting a raid on the horse ranch.

To give some suggestion of legitimacy, old Marshal Tom Cope, always malleable in the hands of the Peace Commission, rode with the raiders because the ostensive reason for the raid was the apprehension of Bert Flinders for the farcical bank robbery attempt engineered by Tuke and his men. Additionally, the raiders wanted to put an end to the menace represented by the two lean saddle tramps who had shown up and were believed to be the Flinders's hired gunhawks.

At rock bottom, there was a reason for the raid which was the private agenda of Nate Sturgis and Bull Tuke. They had their own plans, carefully concealed from the citizens of Vinegar Peak who accompanied them.

They were out to destroy the W-Bar-F and if Will or Bert Flinders should perish in what Sturgis, Tuke and their henchmen planned for the ranch, it would be to the great satisfaction of the boss of Vinegar Peak. High on their priorities were the two supposed professional gunfighters. They posed a danger of unknown calibre. The Vinegar Peak men knew nothing of their background and believed they might well have reputations marked by notches cut into their guns. Sturgis had emphasised that they should be eliminated at the first opportunity.

The moving mass of riders quickened its pace as Nate Sturgis waved his hand to stir them into a trot and they flowed like an ominous stream into the basin, heading towards the panorama of the W-Bar-F with its house, outbuidings, corralled horses and ponies and loose animals at graze in the pastures.

The moon slithered out from the thin desert clouds and Will Flinders, standing on the gallery of the house, saw the intruders coming. He snatched up his Winchester and pumped its lever.

He gave a loud, urgent yell: 'Boys, get your guns! We've got trouble!'

It carried across the yard, alerting the men in the bunkhouse and bringing Walt Harris out of the cook shack where he was preparing supper, buckling on his shellbelt as he ran.

Dannehar, Oskin and the rest of the W-Bar-F hands came out of the bunkhouse at a run and spilled into the ranch yard just as the riders fanned out in front of the buildings. Some, at the direction of Sturgis, halted near a small grove of live oaks a short distance from the house. Dismounting, they hastened into the cover of the trees. The moonlight gave the W-Bar-F men in the yard a full view of them and, with guns primed, they stood their ground, noting the raiders' strategy of detaching a group into the live oaks.

The rest of the raiders pulled rein and halted line abreast, facing the rail fence fronting the ranch house. Marshal Tom Cope, prompted by Sturgis, proceeded with the brief act of theatre that would give the raiders' action some semblance of lawfulness.

In a wavering voice as if not too sure of himself, the lawman called: 'Bert Flinders, this is a posse of the citizens of Vinegar Peak out to arrest you for an attempted robbery at their bank. I'm calling on you to give yourself into custody!'

This caused Bert Flinders's pugnacious spirit to rise. Standing in the yard with his carbine levelled, he yelled: 'Be damned to you, Cope! This is no posse. You've come looking for trouble and, by God, you're going to get it! I'm not surrendering to you!'

As soon as he shouted his defiance, he crouched low with his Winchester tilted and levelled at the horsemen on the other side of the yard fence while, on the gallery, Will Flinders dropped, lay flat and sighted his carbine at the mounted intruders.

In the yard, as if acting on a signal, Oskin,

Dannehar and the W-Bar-F men sought whatever cover was nearest: they crouched behind the long wooden water trough, the water butts and the corners of various buildings.

There was a climbing tension in the air, then the harsh unmistakeable voice of Nate Sturgis bellowed: 'Let 'em have it, men!'

The raiders had planned their opening gambit in advance and there was a crashing volley from the men in the stand of trees which stood to one side of the yard, giving a clear field of fire past the mounted men.

Bullets whanged through the air, striking shards off the wooden structure of the house outbuildings. The men in the ranch yard crouched or lay flat behind their various points of cover but Walt Harris received a burning graze to his left arm while old Harry Scott gave vent to colourful sentiments as his hat was holed.

Then the strategy of the raiding party was revealed when the mounted men before the house spurred their mounts and began to gallop off as if to make a circuit of the ranch while those in the cover of the trees sniped at the men in the yard from their position. They intended to engage the W-Bar-T men while the faction on horseback set about mischief on the side of the yard, shielded from the defenders by the ranch buildings.

Led by Nate Sturgis, the body of riders pounded

around the fenced-in yard, reined up when Sturgis gave a harsh command. Then Sturgis, Bull Tuke and a couple of the men, who had tasted the rough attentions of Dannehar and Oskin in the scuffle in Vinegar Peak, quickly left their saddles. Sturgis took a canister from behind his saddle and with a vicious, throaty chuckling, began to pour kerosene on the coarse grass around the base of the fence.

In the ranch yard, the W-Bar-F men were exchanging shots with the raiders in the trees, a couple of whom showed themselves briefly in the moonlight. Dannehar and Oskin, wielding Winchesters, rose up swiftly from the shelter of the water trough and loosed two barking shots, causing one man to drop and the other to yelp and scoot back into the trees.

In the yard, Bert Flinders was hunkered down against a fence post with his carbine, answering the firing from the trees every time he saw a blaze of muzzle-flame from that quarter. His brother, lying on the gallery of the house was, likewise, keeping up answering fire. Bob Trickett and Walt Harris were established at different corners of the house, shooting with Colts; Harry Scott was behind a water butt with a Smith & Wesson, while Pedro Ruiz fired a Henry rifle from around the corner of the bunkhouse.

The mounted men were a mixed bunch, some

with no experience as horse soldiers, and they were motivated by a species of mob violence – but they had managed to keep themselves together in a solid body behind Nate Sturgis. They were on the blind side of the defenders in the yard and Bull Tuke, with his two hard cases, climbed over the fence and made for the corrals which contained the horses and ponies, now milling and bucking in alarm because of the constant crashing of gunfire. The men opened the gates of the corrals and hastened back to their horses.

Then Nate Sturgis stooped, operated a clumsy flint and wheel lighter and fired the kerosene soaked grass close to the yard fence. Yellow flames flared up at once.

Gunsmoke hung in a pall between the combatants in the ranch yard, and those men in the stand of live oaks and in the yard became conscious of a more pungent quality of smoke adding to the blue drift from the guns.

It was accompanied by an ominous crackling sound and then came the neighing and whinnying of panicking horses and the shuffle and trampling of hoofs.

Pedro Ruiz, stationed at a corner of the bunkhouse, was nearest the fire, spotted the flickering light of the flames first and was soon enveloped by the thickening volume of dark smoke. Leaving his post, he backed into the yard and, through a mask of smoke, he saw the fence rails afire. Moreover, the corral gates were open and the frightened horses were moving in a panic stricken tide, escaping from the pens with some even jumping the corral rails and the yard fence. Coughing and spluttering, Ruiz managed to shout a hoarse warning.

'Fire! Fire! They've started a fire and the stock is escaping!'

On the blind side of the ranch yard, obscured from the W-Bar-F's defenders by the outbuildings, Nate Sturgis was regaining his saddle. Smoke swirled around him and the yellow and crimson of the flames painted his black whiskered face with garish highlights. He growled and spat as the smoke from the burning wood and grass irritated his throat and he croaked to the squad of riders: 'Get back! Ride back! The Flinders want trouble so give it to 'em! Watch out for those gun packing trail tramps and go for them before they get you!'

The horsemen wheeled about and charged off out of the lee of the ranch buildings, coming into sight of the yard. To the men in the Flinders' yard, they were jumbled ghosts in an ever gathering blanket of smoke. Nate Sturgis, taking no chances, was careful to forsake the place at their head and keep the body of riders between the defenders in the yard and himself.

Although it was difficult to define targets and,

with every man fighting for breath and coughing in the choking smoke, the riders loosed a volley of ill aimed fire into the ranch yard as they passed it and the W-Bar-F's foremen, Bob Trickett, dropped lifeless to the ground. Dannehar and Oskin were standing now, blazing away with their carbines through the obscuring blanket. They saw one ghostly horseman throw up his arms and fall backwards into the swirling gloom.

The horseback raiders became dimmer as the volume of smoke intensified but they were obviously in retreat on horses grown fractious with fear. The animals were straining, lurching and snorting in jumbled confusion, trying to find clearer air.

In many of the retreating riders, a change in psychology was taking place. They had followed Nate Sturgis's lead, having had their ire pumped up to near blood lust level by his haranguing against the Flinders brothers and their allies. Now, after witnessing the level of his villainy and taking casualties, they were having second thoughts.

Some, without military backgrounds, found riding into bullet-bitten danger was a stomach churning experience by no means to their taste. Others, veterans of Civil War service on one side or the other, found that the blasting of gunfire, the billowing palls of smoke and the screeching of frightened horses awakened half-forgotten and chilling memories of the horrors of Antietam,

Fredericksburg or Gettysburg. They were learning once again that life as a tradesman or storekeeper was infinitely preferable to soldiering.

The morale of the raiding party was beginning to disintegrate. And no one had yet put paid to those worrying bogeys, the pair who were supposed to be the Flinders's hired gunsharps.

Meanwhile, the loose stock from the W-Bar-F corrals was running in panic as the fire in the yard spread from the fence to the bunkhouse. The deliberately opened corrals allowed the otherwise segregated stallions, mares, colts and ponies to run together in a torrent of horseflesh, screeching and whinnying in white-eyed terror.

Will Flinders came through the fogged yard, shouting in a half choked voice : 'Save the horses! And get those in the stable out before they burn to death!' He ran to the stable building some distance behind the bunkhouse, with his brother, Dannehar and Oskin joining him.

The stables were not yet alight, but the smell of fire and the panic outside had unnerved the horses belonging to the hands, including those of Dannehar and Oskin, housed there. They lurched and kicked in their stalls, braying and snorting.

The remarkably lithe figure of old Harry Scott, noted as a top hand horse wrangler, came streaking in behind the others.

'We've got to save the stock,' he yelled. 'Got to

round 'em up before they run all to hell. I'm going after 'em!' He grabbed his own horse in its stall, calmed its panic and began to mount it bare backed. 'No time to saddle up!' he called to the incredulous four watching him. He kicked his heels into the animal's ribs and sent it galloping out into the foggy chaos of the yard with Scott clinging to its mane and riding without a saddle with the skill of an Indian.

Dannehar and Oskin, calming their own horses, saw the urgency of the situation. Though there were hazards in riding without saddles and rig, Dannehar led his horse out of its stall and emulated Scott, mounting with difficulty.

'Harry's right. I'm going with him,' he yelled.

'Then I'll join you,' responded Slim Oskin as he urged his animal free of its stall. He went through the clumsy business of mounting without stirrups or saddle, kicked his heels and wheeled the horse by manipulating its mane and followed Danneher who had sped out of the stable, jogging awkwardly but retaining his seat. The pair left the Flinders brothers feverishly wrestling the other horses loose from their stalls.

Outside, a portion of the bunkhouse was blazing and, in the smoke shrouded yard, Pedro Ruiz was furiously working the pump beside the water trough, filling a bucket while Walt Harris was at the bunkhouse throwing water from another bucket on the flames. The corpse of Bob Trickett, the foreman, lay in the yard.

The raiders had gone, some satisfied that they had dealt the recalcitrant W-Bar-F a lethal blow and others disturbed and less easy with the night's work.

Out on the ranch's pasturelands, a ragged tide of animals was running in collective panic, streaming away from the frightening fire at the ranch. Other animals that had been grazing loose were catching the fear like an infection and charging alongside the main herd. Striving to reach the head of the herd, riding bareback like a veteran circus performer, Harry Scott clutched the mane of his mount and thanked the powers that be for the natural affinity that had grown up between himself and the animal. It obeyed his urgings without need of a rein. His plan was to run the animals until they were out of the fearsome proximity of the fire and exhaustion slowed them.

Dannehar and Oskin, riding with more difficulty, came pounding up behind him. The old horse wrangler turned, saw them and yelled: 'Try to keep 'em in line. Whip in the stragglers!'

The operation took on something of the techniques of a cattle drive as Dannehar and Oskin went after horses and troublesome young colts who persisted in running out of line. They chased them in, whooping and waving their hats while

51

clinging precariously with one hand to their horses' manes and bouncing on their broad backs, acutely and painfully aware of their lack of saddles.

It was a tricky business for the pair to keep on their horses and turn and wheel the animals as they chased and drove stragglers back into the body of the moving herd but they persevered, in spite of almost being unhorsed more than once. Slowly, steaming and snorting, the tide of horse-flesh slowed its pace. In the fitful moonlight, it became more orderly as it took its lead from a powerful stallion who had naturally taken its place at the head of the herd. Something like natural discipline took hold of the animals.

'Good,' shouted Harry Scott. 'They'll be easier to handle now. Keep 'em moving the way they're going.'

The pace became easier and Dannehar and Oskin, with all the stragglers gathered in, rode beside the herd like outriders on a cattle drive – if less comfortable. The first crimson and gold of desert dawn began to streak the sky and when the riders looked back, they could see the fire at the W-Bar-F, obviously not yet quenched.

The herd of horses was now travelling at a walk and Harry Scott, who seemed to be as accustomed to riding bareback as with a saddle, turned his mount and rode back to Dannehar and Oskin.

'Shouldn't we turn 'em and head back to the

ranch?' Oskin asked.

'No,' said Scott. 'We'll get 'em to water. That'll help tame 'em. There's a canyon with a stream ahead. They call it Ghost Canyon.'

CHAPTER FIVE

AFTERMATH

The widening dawn showed Ghost Canyon to be a steep sided cleft in the range of rocky formations that towered to one side of the fertile basin in which the W-Bar-F nestled. A stream, bordered by sufficient greenery to afford grazing for the horse herd, meandered through it and on one wall there climbed a series of caves fronted by crumbling adobe additions, to make the abandoned dwellings of Indians. Their tribe was now lost to history and old legends clinging to the place had it that their ghosts had possession of the canyon and might be heard in the dark of the moon and when the wind was high.

Harry Scott, Dannehar and Oskin herded the now pacified horses into the canyon. They went easily, attracted by the water and needed little management by the men.

'I reckon we saved most of the stock,' said Scott. 'Any stragglers left out yonder can be rounded up later. They'll be content here and we can leave 'em for a spell and go back to the ranch – if anything is left of it. That fire looked like it was fit to spread.'

Leaving the horses crowding at the stream and drinking, the three mounted their lathered, bare backed animals, which were showing their weariness after their exertions, and they made a laboured wayfaring over a landscape beginning to warm under the climbing sun.

They saw smoke smudging the horizon and the pungency of burnt wood was evident well before they reached the W-Bar-F. They arrived wearily and found Will and Bert Flinders, Pedro Ruiz and Walt Harris in the ravaged yard. The fires were out but a portion of the bunkhouse had been reduced to blackened timbers; flames had damaged one corner of the house and large portions of the yard fence and rails of the corrals were burned to charred remnants. The four who were left at the ranch were near exhaustion through fighting the fires throughout the night. Their faces were blackened, their clothing scorched and Walt Harris had a roughly bandaged arm.

Scarves of smoke lingered over the scene, giving it a forlorn aspect where, so short a time before, it had looked smart and prosperous but the Flinders brothers, Ruiz and Harris stood in the midst of the devastation looking as doggedly defiant as ever.

Dannehar, Oskin and Scott greeted them with the news that the bulk of the ranch's stock had been saved and was safely grazing at Ghost Canyon.

The brothers were serious faced. 'They got Bob Trickett,' reported Will. 'Shot clean through the head. We took his body into the house. If we finished off any of their bunch, they must have taken the corpses with 'em. We looked in the trees and found blood on the ground but no bodies.'

His brother grunted. 'We got some all right. I saw more than one fall and I figure we made some widows in Vinegar Peak but if a town turns plumb poison it'll have to suffer the consequences. I guess you saw who was leading them.'

'Sure, Nate Sturgis. He must have worked up Vinegar Peak's dander to a hell of a pitch. I saw some in that bunch I'd never call fighting men,' said Bert Flinders. 'Darned if I don't almost feel sorry for old Tom Cope, the way he was pulled in to make it look as if they had lawful reason for riding against us.'

'They only had one reason and that was to ruin us,' his brother said. 'Judging by the faces I saw among that bunch, it seems every man in Vinegar Peak is against us.'

'It looks like the whole thing was done for Black Eagle's benefit and with the intention of burning you out completely,' Dannehar said. 'Deploying a bunch to snipe at us from the trees to keep us busy while the rest went off and set the fire was a pretty slick trick. It shows the attack was well planned beforehand.'

Bert Flinders growled defiantly: 'They haven't licked us and, if I have my way, they never will so long as there's an inch of W-Bar-F land left to stand on. We still have plenty of ammunition left and I'll get back at 'em so long as I have a last bullet. After that, I'll use my bare hands!'

'Calm down,' advised his brother. 'We have to think about burying Bob Trickett. Like many a man in this Territory, Bob never talked about where he came from or if he had any kin. You know how things are out here. If a man shows he'd rather keep his secrets, you don't pester him. All I know is he was a damned good foreman and a damned good man. He deserves a funeral at Cemetery Ridge, with the preacher officiating but, if any of us ride into town, we'd be poking our noses into the rattlesnake's nest. The best we can give Bob is a cowpoke's funeral with a gunnysack for his coffin. I reckon we should bury him yonder near the trees. There's a secluded spot there that'll be suitable for a grave.'

Later that morning, a short journey was made to

the grove of trees that had sheltered the snipers the night before. The body of the foreman, wrapped in a gunnysack, was borne on the ranch's buck-board. Pedro Ruiz and Walt Harris each carried a spade and they began to dig in the selected location.

Bob Trickett was lowered into his last resting place and, for five minutes, his colleagues stood around the grave, hatless and in quiet dignity. Then earth was shovelled into the grave and the party walked back to the stricken ranch, leading the buck-board.

Surveying the damage at the ranch, Will Flinders said: 'It seems like we're almost starting again. The loss of those corrals is a hell of a blow and it'll take time to replace them and to repair the bunkhouse and the part of the house that's damaged. And we have to think about keeping the stock intact.'

Old Harry Scott was thoughtful. 'We can keep 'em penned up where they are in Ghost Canyon by throwing a barrier or a picket fence across the entrance,' he said. 'There's graze and water enough in the canyon. They'll be safe there until we get things fixed here. We left them settled down well enough and I reckon I have enough horse savvy to know when cayuses are content.'

'Seems like a reasonable enough solution,' Will Flinders said. 'There's no question of allowing ourselves to go under because of Sturgis and his gang. We'll get some rest, then set to work. We've still got an outfit to run and we'll sure as shooting do it!'

'And a war to fight – against the whole of Vinegar Peak,' said Cephas Dannehar.

That same morning, Vinegar Peak was also living with the aftermath of the night raid. Many of those who rode with Nate Sturgis were now wondering how they had been persuaded to take up arms against the Flinders brothers and their allies. In several cases, consciences had been severely disturbed. The more thoughtful saw that they had been swept along by a form of mass hysteria even though they could not bring themselves to admit it out loud.

Then there was the cost, a factor that concentrated the mind of more than one citizen. The defenders of the ranch fought with consistent accuracy from good cover and had taken the lives of four raiders and wounded three.

Nate Sturgis had insisted on following an Indian tactic and carrying off his dead. In his devious scheming, he saw that he might exploit their deaths as sacrifices made in the cause of civic virtue against those who would hinder the material progress of Vinegar Peak. The wounded, too, might be portrayed as good citizens injured in defence of their community's good.

In the undisciplined scramble to get away from

the burning ranch, Sturgis, Bull Tuke and others of the Peace Commission's squad of riders had picked up the four corpses – two from the grove of live oaks and two from the fighting in front of the W-Bar-F yard – and rode with them slung across their saddle pommels. The victims were Dave Cullen, a somewhat hotheaded carpenter from the town, two Black Eagle miners and one of the Peace Commission riders, a surly ruffian named Hank Graham. Cullen was married but childless and Sturgis considered that he might be portrayed as a martyr to the villainy of the Flinders brothers who stood in the way of Vinegar Peak's advancement and who had brought two professional gunfighters into the locality.

He thought he might also exploit the plight of Cullen's widow as a further emotional weapon in his vendetta against the W-Bar-F. But, in that, he was disappointed. When the riders returned to town with Cullen's body, his widow, a tough, raw-boned woman moulded by the frontier, seemed hardly to care. It seemed the Cullens' marriage lacked tender sentiment and it was even suspected that Mrs Cullen was glad to be rid of her spouse.

The remaining three of the dead: the miners and Graham, the Peace Commission hard case, were frontier drifters whose background was a blank and they were not known to have anyone to mourn their passing.

A hasty funeral party was arranged on the afternoon of the return to the town. The corpses were interred at Cemetery Ridge, the stark, grave studded rise on the edge of town. Old Levi Tibbins, the town's preacher, said a few appropriate words. Nate Sturgis tried to get into full flow with a speech about noble souls dying while exercising the right of citizens to purge their community of social evil but he saw that he was no longer stirring warlike emotions so he never reached the height of his usual blowhard oratory.

Then there were the three who arrived home with flesh wounds which kept Doc Furey, Vinegar Peak's only medico, busy. Far from feeling like heroes, all three, in the deeper recesses of their consciousness, reflected on the point that they went in en masse against inferior numbers and still came off badly when faced by the staunch defence of the W-Bar-F men. So far as anyone knew, the threatening question of the two imported gunfighters had not been settled.

Marshal Tom Cope, who was largely a passenger in the raid and who knew he had been used to spearhead the action, made himself inconspicuous, keeping out of sight in his office and secretly sharing the qualms of unease that were stirring in the body politic of Vinegar Peak.

Late in the afternoon, four riders appeared in Vinegar Peak's single street. They came out of the

Globe Creek country in southern Arizona. They were the substantial figure of Chad Bellingham, accompanied by his foreman, Lute Stevens and a couple of hands, Dan Cox and Red Salter. Bellingham, a veteran rancher, had built up a cattle spread of fair size since the end of the Civil War. There was no nonsense about Old Man Bellingham. He had fought Apaches, cross-border rustlers out of Mexico, drought and cattle sickness in the course of establishing his Circle B outfit. Now he was going through a prosperous time and was out to improve his remuda of horses.

He had traded with Will Flinders in the past and he was in the course of visiting the W-Bar-F to make more purchases.

Intent on breaking their journey for food more satisfying than trail rations, the four rode horses dusty with hard travelling into Vinegar Peak and headed directly for Seth Rogan's restaurant, where they had stopped on previous visits.

They dismounted and hitched their animals at the rack in front of the eating house. Chad Bellingham led the way and the party entered the restaurant with ringing spurs. Bellingham was a big man, almost as broad as he was tall, with a beak of a nose overshadowing the droopy crescent of a huge walrus moustache. He was known far and wide among Arizona cattlemen and Seth Rogan, leaning on the counter in his empty restaurant, straightened up when the rancher and his three employees entered.

'Good afternoon, Mr Bellingham,' he greeted deferentially. 'Good to see you gentlemen in Vinegar Peak again. What'll it be?'

Rogan was an obese man not noted for physical exertion. He served up good food but he was of sly disposition and a supporter of the Peace Commission so he had the veneer of a solid citizen. He was not on the previous night's raid partly because he was no horseman but chiefly because he lacked fighting guts. He was, however, fully in favour of the scheming of Nate Sturgis and the Black Eagle satellites to oust the Flinders brothers from the W-Bar-F and put the projected railroad through their land.

'Plenty of beef, potatoes and gravy for me and the boys and plenty of coffee,' stipulated Chad Bellingham.

'Sure thing, Mr Bellingham. Right away,' said Rogan as he scooted into the back premises where his wife toiled over the cooking.

He returned promptly with a tray bearing plates piled high with steaming food and a large coffee pot.

'You back in this country on business, Mr Bellingham?' he asked as he laid out the food on the table at which Bellingham, Stevens, Cox and Salter had taken their seats.

'Why else?' grunted the rancher. 'We're here to buy horseflesh from the W-Bar-F.'

Seth Rogan, who had anticipated the answer, gave a crooked grin. 'That might prove difficult, sir,' he said. 'It seems Will Flinders's outfit has run into some trouble. No telling whether it's in any fit condition to trade.' There was a suggestion of glee in his manner.

Old Man Bellingham laid down his knife. 'How so?' he asked. 'We've heard nothing of any difficulties.'

Seth Rogan went cautiously. Like all Vinegar Peak, he knew plenty about the raid but he had no intention of saying too much to Bellingham who was known to be friendly towards Will Flinders and his brother. 'Well, it seems they were raided last night by some unknown persons and their stock was driven off and scattered all to hell,' he said. 'I've only heard rumours but there's no telling if they can muster any cayuses at all. Could be you've come a long way for nothing.'

'Raided?' Bellingham said. 'Who raided? Not Apaches; they've settled down and you're too far from the border for Mexican rustlers. Maybe you've got home-grown horse rustlers in this country.'

Rogan put on the pose of knowing very little about the raid which was currently adopted by much of Vinegar Peak but, in his case, the wilful ignorance was unaccompanied by the creeping guilt felt by many townspeople. 'Can't say but rumour has it that the W-Bar-F was also set afire in the raid.' He gave a mock sigh of concern. 'Sure is hard on the Flinders.'

Old Man Bellingham scowled and resumed his eating. He was a cattleman with a cattleman's suspicion of other businesses that sought to crowd the cowmen off their ranges on the plea of progress. He had long heard ugly tales about Nate Sturgis and Vinegar Peak's Peace Commission and its backing by interests opposed to those of the cattlemen. The four ate in silence, then Bellingham jerked his head towards the door. 'C'mon, boys,' he said. 'Let's ride. I'm plumb anxious to know how things are at the W-Bar-F. And there's something about this damned town that makes me want to shake its dust off my boots!'

CHAPTER SIX

MAN ON THE PROD

Old Man Bellingham and his three companions rode into the basin and, from a distance, stared in horror at the scene of charred and blackened destruction visible at the W-Bar-F ranch. On arrival, they found the Flinders brothers with Walt Harris and two lean strangers busily tidying the yard although all showed the weariness brought on by the strain of the previous night's events.

As the four visitors swung out of their saddles, Will and Bert Flinders walked over to them with surprise registered on their faces. The brothers greeted Chad Bellingham with a handshake. 'We sure didn't expect anyone aiming to do business today. As you can see, we're at a kind of disadvantage.'

'Yeah, we heard you were raided,' said the veteran rancher. 'We heard in Vinegar Peak that it was by unknown persons and your stock was run off.'

'Oh, we know who was responsible, all right. So does the whole of Vinegar Peak since it was pretty much the whole blamed town that turned against us,' Will Flinders said. 'It's a long story but we have stock aplenty, all safely gathered at Ghost Canyon just a hoot and holler away. Harry Scott and Pedro Ruiz are out there right now, attending to the cayuses. You haven't had a wasted journey no matter what they told you in Vinegar Peak. We're more than ready to do business. What're you needing?'

'Ponies, suitable for cutting out work. Good, sturdy critters, same as you've supplied in the past,' stated Old Man Bellingham. 'Something like twenty head of 'em.'

'We can fill that bill,' said Will Flinders with enthusiasm. 'We have ponies with enough mustang in 'em to make 'em ideal for cutting out. I'll ride over to Ghost Canyon with you and you can select the ones you fancy. I'll leave these boys to carry on with the work. We're trying to make fast progress just to show we're not beaten. I'll tell you about what's been happening here as we ride.'

Will Flinders went into the stable to rig his horse and Harris, Dannehar and Oskin continued clearing the debris while Chad Bellingham and his companions watered their horses at the trough, replenished since its contents were used to fight the fire.

When Will Flinders led his horse from the stable, he joined the group at the trough and addressed Old Man Bellingham. 'I reckon you'll aim to move off with the ponies tomorrow,' he said. 'We'll rustle up some grub later and, between the house and what's left of the bunkhouse, we can offer you sleeping accommodation for the night if you don't mind a little inconvenience.'

'Much obliged. That'll suit us fine,' said Bellingham. 'We've got our bedrolls with us and we slept under the stars last night. I reckon we'll get a better night's sleep here with no inconvenience about it.'

Will Flinders and the visitors from the Circle B mounted up and rode for Ghost Canyon with Flinders knowing a sense of elation at the prospect of business so soon after the W-Bar-F's setback.

Dannehar, Oskin and Walt Harris joined Bert Flinders near the charred gateposts at the yard's opening and watched them depart.

Looking thoughtful, Bert Flinders said: 'It's a good thing Old Man Bellingham showed up just when we need a boost of confidence. He's good for business and we need to feel our heads are still above water. I guess he and his men will be riding through Vinegar Peak with a string of ponies and darned if I haven't a notion to ride with them just to show that blasted town the W-Bar-F is still kicking, still in business and producing prime horseflesh.'

Dannehar noted that, in spite of his tiredness, the younger Flinders was showing something of his old reckless spirit. 'That'd be plumb foolish,' he said. 'You were warned once before about going into the rattlesnake's nest. Things will be a damned sight more dangerous now. The raiders didn't finish you off last night but there are plenty in town who would try to as soon as they saw you.'

Bert Flinders gave his familiar devil-be-damned laugh and his eyes glittered determinedly. 'Let 'em try. Maybe they'll give me an excuse to get even for the killing of Bob Trickett and I'd welcome it,' he said. 'I liked Bob and I've had a hankering to see him have justice ever since we carried his body to the grave. Apart from that, I'd like to ride in just to cock a snook at Sturgis, the Peace Commission and all Vinegar Peak.'

'The odds are against you.' Oskin said. 'And you could be bringing the Circle B men in on our fight if shooting starts. Hell, Sturgis has the whole town riled up against us and they're out to get you for that lying bank robbery yarn. We'd best all think coolly and act in a body when action is needed – and it sure will be soon enough.'

Bert Flinders shrugged but the rebellious gleam was still in his eyes. Both Dannehar and Oskin noted it. It was something they knew from his days of army scouting at Fort Truelove – and it always meant trouble to come.

Just as the sun was lowering, Will Flinders, Bellingham, Stevens, Cox and Salter returned to the ranch. The Circle B men had selected their preferred ponies at Ghost Canyon, where the animals were left with Harry Scott and Pedro Ruiz, who were bedding down for the night there. They were to bring the animals to the W-Bar-F the following morning ready to be taken on the trail by Old Man Bellingham and the Circle B men.

With their tidying chores complete and Walt Harris having busied himself in the cook shack, the party settled down to a meal in the living room of the damaged house.

'Could be we're taking a chance, leaving Harry and Pedro at the canyon all night. If there's another raid tonight, we're two defenders short,' Will Flinders said as they ate.

Chad Bellingham gave a rumbling laugh. 'You're not short of man power while my boys and me are here. Darned if I wouldn't welcome a brawl. Things have been awful quiet in the Globe Creek country for a long time. I've taken a dislike to Vinegar Peak and its folk since hearing about last night's ruction. I reckon my boys ain't about to

70

run away from trouble either.'

'Nothing so sure, Boss,' chuckled his foreman, Lute Stevens, helping himself to more potatoes. 'Sometimes I hanker for the smell of powder-smoke and the sound of bullets. They remind me of my misspent youth!'

The night passed without trouble though the party took the precaution of keeping weapons ready while the brothers with Dannehar and Oskin, kept two hourly turns on watch and the Circle B men slept, preparatory to their long journey the following day.

At the crack of dawn, Harry Scott and Pedro Ruiz arrived from Ghost Canyon driving twenty head of spirited ponies none of which had suffered in the panic during the raid. They rounded up the animals into a bunch in front of the ranch yard and Chad Bellingham and his companions, having breakfasted, mounted up and rode out to take them on the trail.

Old Man Bellingham waved his hat in farewell to the W-Bar-F men. 'Thanks for the hospitality,' he called. 'I'll put the word around the cowmen at my end of the Territory that the W-Bar-F is still in business and still raising the best horseflesh.'

Will Flinders watched the party move off in a cloud of dust with a feeling of satisfaction. His outfit had suffered a vicious blow from Nate Sturgis and his Vinegar Peak cohorts but it had just made a valuable sale to one of the most prominent cattlemen in Arizona Territory and its reputation was still good.

The W-Bar-F crew, plus Dannehar and Oskin gathered in the house to consider the outfit's present and future problems and how they might be remedied. Assessing the damage, Will Flinders observed that it was up to themselves to tackle the necessary repairs.

'Vinegar Peak is poisoned against us so we can't venture into town to find a carpenter,' he said. 'Looks like there's a permanent state of war between that damned town and us from here on in. When it comes to getting supplies and such, we're going to have to trek over to Blue Mesa and that's a tolerable ride.'

Walt Harris suddenly noticed that Bert Flinders was missing. He was last seen something like twenty minutes before but now he seemed to have slipped away.

Cephas Dannehar, recalling the well remem- bered signs of determination in the younger brother's eyes, ran to the stable and hastened back.

'His horse has gone,' he reported. 'Looks like he slid away and took his cayuse and walked it off quietly while we were in the house. And you know what that means.'

'Sure,' said Oskin. 'He's gone off to catch up

with Old Man Bellingham to ride through Vinegar Peak with him and cock a snook at the whole damned town. He talked about it.'

'The damned hotheaded fool!' exploded Will Flinders. 'That's just the kind of loco thing he would do and he'll get plenty of trouble if he goes into town. He knows the whole place is gunning for him.'

'He has an ulterior motive,' Dannahar said. 'He wants to show that the W-Bar-F is still kicking, but I reckon, more than that, he's pretty well on the prod to avenge Bob Trickett's death. He said so earlier. He always had reckless guts but this time he's up against odds stacked well over his head. If he goes into town he'll never get out alive.'

'I'm going after him,' growled Will Flinders. 'He'll hardly have caught up with Old Man Bellingham yet. If he gets into a shooting scrape in their company, he'll endanger the Circle B men and the ponies.'

The older brother moved for the door quickly and Dannehar and Oskin followed on his heels.

'We'll come with you,' said Dannehar. 'And we'll have to ride like all hell!'

CHAPTER SEVEN

GUNSMOKE IN THE SCRUBLAND

Bert Flinders paced his horse at a smart clip along the trail to Vinegar Peak. His well known rebel streak had become irked at the prospect of putting in hours of repair work at the W-Bar-F and discussing the next stage of the ranch's feud with Nate Sturgis, the Black Eagle mine, the Peace Commission and all of Vinegar Peak. He wanted action and his restless spirit drove him to the trail on an errand of his own though he knew his colleagues at the W-Bar-F would see it as reckless almost to the point of insanity.

He was out to catch up with Old Man Bellingham and his string of ponies just to have the pleasure of riding through Vinegar Peak with them to show the citizens of that perverse town that the horse ranch had not been knocked flat by the raid; that its stock had not been scattered and lost and that the W-Bar-F was doing business with no less an outfit than the Circle B. There would be exquisite pleasure in seeing the folk of the town gawp open mouthed as he accompanied the Circle B owner and his trail crew to the far end of town. Although he knew many hands were against him, he was relatively sure that no one would take action against him when in the company of so august an Arizona pioneer as Chad Bellingham.

Returning could be a different matter. He aimed to part company with the Circle B crew having passed through the town and deliberately make his way back along the main street instead of riding in a wide loop around the town.

On this lone journey, he might easily meet with trouble and he would almost welcome it. The odds would be uneven, but if the Vinegar Peak citizenry wanted a shooting affray, Bert Flinders was willing to take them on. He would indeed be plunging into a rattlesnake's nest but he'd done so many times before, even against so formidable a set of adversaries as warring Apaches, and come out with a whole skin.

An exchange of bullets might give him a chance to even the score for the shooting of the W-Bar-F's

75

foreman, Bob Trickett. The truth about head-strong Bert Flinders was that he had never outlived a natural youthful ebullience and believed he bore a charmed life.

Now his horse pounded the trail some distance behind Old Man Bellingham's party and some miles short of Vinegar Peak. On his heels, forcing speed out of lathered mounts, came his brother with Dannehar and Oskin, all three of whom were unconvinced of his charmed existence and were racing to save him from plunging headlong into disaster.

The younger Flinders had no idea that he was being followed by the determined trio as he traversed a stretch of scrub, scattered boulders and tumbleweeds. He approached a humped group of sun split boulders around which the trail snaked; he rounded the boulders and saw four distant horsemen ahead of him on the trail and heading towards him. Even from a distance, he saw that they were Peace Commission riders and leading them was the unmistakable bearded figure of Bull Tuke.

He acted with the speed that had saved his life in his affrays with the Apaches. He hunched low in the saddle, reined back his horse, shucked his stir-rups and dropped to the ground. Holding his reins, he raced back into the high boulders behind him, bringing the animal into their cover. Clearing his Colt from leather, he squatted behind a boulder and watched the four riders. They had put on a spurt of speed, having obviously spotted him and recognized him. Bull Tuke took the lead and the sun flashed briefly on the metal of his six-gun as he drew it.

Bert Flinders cocked his own weapon and waited. He watched the riders approach and fan out, putting space between each other, obviously realizing that, bunched together, they made too easy a target for Flinders who had an open field of fire.

Bull Tuke loosed a wild shot and the bullet chipped a boulder close to Flinders's head.

Tuke's companions, continuing to ride forward, began to fire into the boulders and Flinders crouched low as the bullets snarled around his cover. He raised his head over the boulder, fired a couple of shots and saw that the four were taking no chances out on the open scrubland. They had halted and dismounted, and were hauling their horses to their knees, intending to fire from a lying position.

Lying, they found cover behind clumps of scrub and rocks and Flinders was left with only the positions of their visible hats to fire at. He let fly with a handful of shots and, while answering slugs spanged off the boulders, he hunkered down and replenished the chambers of his weapon from his shellbelt.

Behind him, a mile or so along the trail from the W-Bar-F, Dannehar, Oskin and Will Flinders heard the shooting from up ahead and automatically spurred their lathered horses.

They raised the dust at a sustained gallop, hearing the exchange of more shots over the pounding of their mounts. They reached the rearing boulders in the path of the trail, saw drifts of gunsmoke over the scrubland and realized that the firing was between persons out in the open and someone holed up in the cluster of boulders near to them.

Bert Flinders's head emerged from behind his cover. He looked in astonishment at the newly arrived riders, recognized them, overcame his surprise and shouted: 'Will, Dannehar, Oskin—' He was cut short by a fusillade of shots from the men out in the scrub which sent hot lead flying around the boulders. Bert Flinders bellowed: 'Quick! Get in here with your cayuses!'

The three speedily left their saddles and scrambled into the boulders, leading their horses.

'What are you doing here?' Bert Flinders asked as the three squatted behind cover and drew their revolvers.

'Trying to save your damnfool skin, you hotheaded halfwit,' shouted his brother. The newcomers joined in the affray, answering shots from the men lying on the scrubland.

'Who's out there?' asked Dannehar.

'Tuke and three of the Peace Commission crew,' said Bert Flinders.

'Hell, you sure stacked up the odds against yourself,' said his brother. 'Four against one and they'd probably wear you down as your ammunition ran out.'

Bert Flinders gave his familiar reckless laugh. 'I've got 'em pinned down. I've got the position of every one of 'em marked and they can't move from their cover.'

There was a rapid succession of shots between the two sets of adversaries during which a yelp of pain was heard from one of the men, sprawling under the meagre cover out on the scrubland. There followed a cessation in the shooting and a bulky figure rose from behind a clump of scrub. The W-Bar-F men holed up in the boulders watched in astonishment, recognizing it as Bull Tuke, holding a Colt .45 and exposing his whole body in spite of the danger.

He began to stride forward through wreaths of powdersmoke, heading determinedly towards the boulders.

With his naked gun half raised, he bellowed: 'Hey, you – the guy who pulled my whiskers – you and your damned sidekick came into this country and caused trouble and I don't care if you are a hotshot gunfighter, I aim to settle with you! Step

79

out from behind those rocks and I'll blast you all to hell!'

There was now a heavy silence over the scrubland and boulders. Bull Tuke was putting the fight on another level, the appearance of Dannehar seeming to have awakened his grudge for the way he had been humiliated in Vinegar Peak. This battle had become a personal matter between Bull Tuke and Cephas Dannehar. The big man had broken cover and the W-Bar-F men had to admit he was showing plenty of guts in walking across the open scrubland towards their position, hooting his challenge.

'Come out!' he roared, still pacing forward steadily.

Dannehar recharged the chambers of his Colt, scrambled over the boulder that had afforded him cover and walked towards Tuke, his right hand gripping his Colt and hanging loosely at his side. He walked on and Tuke continued his progress until there were only yards between the two. Tuke swung up his weapon, pointing its mouth directly at Dannehar's head, and taking steady aim.

'I didn't kill you in the fight at the W-Bar-F but I will now!' he snarled.

'Then get to it,' responded Dannehar flatly. Then his gun hand flashed upwards and his Colt barked. Bull Tuke took the bullet full in the chest, and scooted back on his heels, dropping his gun.

Then he keeled over backwards, dead before he hit the dust.

The echo of Dannehar's shot died and a leaden silence followed which Dannehar expected would be broken at any moment by vengeful firing, catching him in the open but there was only the silence as he turned and walked back to the cover of the boulders. Back in their shelter, he found Flinders and Oskin with their weapons trained on the points from which their adversaries had fired. Tension climbed in the silence.

Suddenly, a hand appeared from behind one of the clumps of brush. It held a dirty white bandana which was waved in the breezeless air.

'Well, by the great horned toad – a flag of truce!' exclaimed Will Flinders.

'Maybe they're admitting they're licked or it could be a trick,' said Slim Oskin.

Will Flinders shouted: 'What do you want?'

A dejected voice issued from behind the brush clump: 'You've killed another of us over here. We want to collect both bodies and get the hell out. There's only two of us left.'

The four behind the boulders levelled their weapons at the speaker's cover and Will Flinders answered harshly: 'All right, but we're keeping you covered. Try any tricks and there'll be none of you left.'

The four watched two clumps of brush twitch as

activity started behind them and, eventually, two range garbed figures arose, each gripping the reins of horses which they had forced to lie under cover and were now being brought to a standing position. One man walked his animal over to a neighbouring tangle of shrubbery from behind which he lifted a still human form. He proceeded to haul the corpse over the horn of the saddle, while his companion led a horse towards the body of Bull Tuke. Hauling the bulky corpse up from the ground cost him a strenuous effort but he, too, managed to drape it over the fore portion of the saddle. He then took the reins and led the burdened animal back to where his companion waited. Together, the pair retrieved the further two horses of the party, mounted and rode in the direction of Vinegar Peak, each leading an animal carrying a human burden.

'Licked 'em,' said Bert Flinders enthusiastically. 'I reckon we've given Sturgis something to think about.'

'And you still put yourself in the damndest position, all because of your fool bravado,' his disapproving brother said. 'Seems like you need tying down for your own good.'

Nate Sturgis already had something to think about even before he was aware of the misfortunes of Bull Tuke and his sidekicks.

About the time that the four Peace Commission riders first sighted Bert Flinders, he stood at a window in his office at the headquarters of the Black Eagle mine and scowled. The window gave him a view of the portion of the main street of Vinegar Peak and he was watching a string of ponies progressing along its rutted length at an easy pace under the eyes of four energetic riders, who kept the animals moving in the manner of cowhands trail-herding beef on the hoof.

The boss of Vinegar Peak needed no telling who the most prominent of the horsemen was. All Arizona Territory knew Chad Bellingham of the Circle B.

It was the second time in two days that Sturgis had laid eyes on the visiting rancher.

The previous day, he'd caught sight of Old Man Bellingham and his companions riding through the town. He quickly learned, thanks to word being passed by the talkative Seth Rogan of the eating house, that Bellingham and his riders were en route to the W-Bar-F to purchase horses.

Now, he was chagrined to see that Bellingham had concluded his business and was returning home with a set of what appeared to be perfectly sound and spirited ponies. Sturgis had hoped that his raid on the horse ranch would have caused such mayhem that the bulk of its stock would be scattered far and wide. Perhaps some animals would have suffered such maiming that Will Flinders and his brother would have been dealt a crippling blow. But obviously, when it came to supplying energetic and hardy animals for working cattle, the W-Bar-F was still in business. Old Man Bellingham would never buy inferior horseflesh.

Sturgis growled into his black whiskers. His raid on the horse ranch, it seemed, had achieved little in the way of daunting the Flinders brothers or putting a dent in their business. It might have damaged the property but the very fact that Bellingham was returning through the town with the ponies seemed a defiant signal that the brothers were staying put and not running scared.

Sturgis reflected on the overall effects of the raid with uneasy feelings.

Vinegar Peak had been quick to unleash mob lust against the brothers whom they saw as holding out against the town's advancement but now he was hearing tales of disgruntlement that too many corpses had been buried in the town's cemetery.

The pair of skinny trail tramps whom Sturgis had represented as hired gunmen troubled him more than ever. So far as he knew, they had survived the raid. His last view of them was of them standing together in the ranch yard, with Winchesters spitting bullets through the swirls of smoke and the dust risen by his panicky horsemen as their raid unravelled. Ever since their advent, all his strategy seemed to have gone wrong and his preconceived notion that a brutal attack on the W-Bar-F would knock the outfit out of action had turned out as substantial as a pipe dream.

Later that morning, his chagrin increased when, into his office came two dusty, range garbed men, trudging with dejected weariness.

Sturgis glared at them. They were two of the Peace Commission riders, hard cases who had been on the raid. Everything about their demeanour boded ill and Sturgis barked: 'Well, what do you want?'

Without ceremony, one, by the name of Hank Marsh, stated: 'Bull Tuke's dead.'

'What?' bellowed Sturgis.

'Shot by one of them gunfighters,' said the second man, named Dave O'Phelim. 'Billy Twist is dead, too. We brought their bodies back. They're down in the yard.'

'How the hell did it happen?' demanded Sturgis.

Hank Marsh began to recite a bitter narrative. 'Tuke, Dave, Billy and me came across Bert Flinders outside town and figured we'd arrest him for that bank robbery he attempted but he scooted back into some boulders and started shooting. We took him on. Then Will Flinders showed up with those two gunsharps. They joined young Flinders in smoking it out with us.

'We were taking what cover we could, then Billy was shot dead. Things quieted down a mite and we were running short on ammunition. We couldn't believe it but Bull Tuke up and called out that gunman who pulled his whiskers. He was mighty sore about it and I figure he reckoned he'd get even for it while he still had some ammunition. I never thought Tuke had that kind of guts but he stepped out of cover and called that guy and he came out of his own cover and—'

'Shot Tuke,' finished Sturgis with a snort. 'Hell, Tuke should have known better than to tackle a gunslinger face to face. He might have known the guy could serve him up for breakfast.'

'And there's something else,' stated Marsh.

'What?' demanded Sturgis.

Marsh jerked his head toward O'Phelim and said: 'Him and me – we're quitting. We've had enough. We're riding over the hill.'

'Yeah, we want our back pay,' O'Phelim said.

'Scared like jackrabbits because of those two gunnies I suppose,' growled Sturgis. 'Well, you'll be paid off. I have no time for gutless *hombres.* You'll get your pay and you can go to hell.'

He glowered after the pair as they left the office and his feelings of unease intensified. The brutish Tuke, a reliable sidekick in his villainous schemes who had played a major part in burning the W-Bar-F headquarters was dead due his unexpected surge of vengeful courage. Once again, the pair of trail tramps had come upon the scene, dealing death; there were troubling rumours of discontent among the townsfolk and, now, two Peace Commission riders were quitting. A contagion seemed to be spreading.

Again, he had the sense that all his plans were going awry and, this time, the feeling was more profound than ever.

He had to do something about it – and quickly!

Then he remembered the town of Skeleton Flat, only half a day's ride away.

CHAPTER EIGHT

GUNSLINGERS
COME CALLING

Wally Drever, Vinegar Peak's blacksmith, was busy before most of the town was awake and he was firing up his forge as early daylight was broadening. He heard the jingle of ring bits and the tramp of a horse issuing from the quiet street and, when he looked out of the door, he saw the intriguing sight of Nate Sturgis on horseback, heading out of town.

It was rare to see the boss of Vinegar Peak active at this hour and just as rare to see him in the saddle at any time. He occupied bachelor quarters at the offices of the mine and most of his day was spent in the offices, dealing with Black Eagle's business. Because the Black Eagle directors were mostly Kansas City based absentees, he was the company's only major representative to be found on the premises.

Wally Drever had a reputation as a tankerous character – one who usually marched out of step with everyone else – but he was as honest as the day was long and straight as a die, which was more than could be said for many of his fellow citizens. He rubbed his chin thoughtfully as he watched the retreating back of the Black Eagle boss.

'He's up to something,' he said to himself.

Since the raid on the Flinders brothers' ranch, Drever had been thinking about the turn of events in the Vinegar Peak country. Only the day before, the town watched breathlessly as the two Peace Commission riders plodded down the street, bringing the corpses of Bull Tuke and Billy Twist. The sight intensified the disgruntled feelings that were increasingly showing themselves in the town.

Very typically, Drever took no part in the raid on the W-Bar-F and he opposed it vocally. Only a couple of days before, Jim Simms, one of his cronies who had gone along with the raiders, had showed up at the forge for a smoke and a chat and Drever tackled him about his involvement.

'To pick on an outfit in force that way was a hell of a thing to do, Jim,' he said. 'Then, damn it, you burned the place. And all because Nate Sturgis prodded you into it.'

'Hell, Wally, don't you start bulldogging me. I'm getting enough trouble from the wife. She keeps harping on the number of people who got themselves killed and says I could have been among them. I figured we were striking a blow for the good of the town and I didn't know there was going to be any burning. I reckon I just got carried along by the rest of 'em.'

'Sure, and a lot of them are telling the same story and are trying to square their consciences,' Drever said. 'There's a heap of guilty feeling in this town. Dick Owens told me that he got sickened when the place began to blaze. He was with Sherman's army when it burned Atlanta and he said that was the one thing in the big war that haunted him. He never agreed with it and the burning at the W-Bar-F brought back all the memories. Dick says he'll think more than twice before he gets tied up in any such thing again. And that's the sort of talk you'll hear all over town.'

'I know it,' admitted Simms. 'Most of us that got suckered into the raid by Sturgis can hardly look each other in the eye. Darned if I don't feel I'm on the Flinders's side now. Maybe they were right to bring in a couple of gunslingers considering the odds stacked against 'em.'

On the morning Nate Sturgis left on horseback, Wally Drever pumped his bellows to redden the coals of the forge and reflected on the mood that was almost tangible in Vinegar Peak.

'Bad consciences,' he said to himself. 'We've got a town full of bad consciences and there's something in the wind, what with Tuke and one of his sidekicks dead, and Sturgis all but sneaking out of town at almost the break of day.'

Nate Sturgis turned westward when he left Vinegar Peak behind and headed off towards the flatlands and wide skies of the desert. He did not like horseback travel but this was one journey he had to take. With the killing of Bull Tuke and Billy Twist and the desertion of Marsh and O'Phelim, he felt the guts were being kicked out of his private collection of toughs and he feared others might throw in their hand now that Tuke, a kingpin of the Peace Commission force, was dead.

The task Sturgis had embarked on was best undertaken personally. Hirelings might no longer be trustworthy.

His objective was Skeleton Flat, a brooding desert edge settlement of sun warped wooden structures and crumbling adobe buildings that dated from earlier Spanish occupation. It might, at first glance, be taken for a ghost town. It had a spotty reputation and it was known that the law was not established there. One never knew just who was residing or taking refuge there, but Nate Sturgis had a reasonable hope of finding one if not both of a pair of specific men.

91

He paced his horse easily under the climbing sun, resting and watering the animal a couple of times at waterholes, and he reached Skeleton Flat just before the noon zenith. At first sight, the place presented a deserted appearance with abandoned looking false fronts and sagging awnings over ill kept plankwalks. One structure stood out because it bore signs of life, of a kind, in the form of several loafers sprawled on chairs under its shaded frontage. It bore the title The Territorial Saloon and the loafers showed a lazy interest in the new-comer who, in his black broadcloth suit with a flashy watch chain, was far from the usual desert traveller.

Sturgis dismounted, looped his rein to a rickety hitching rack, and entered the saloon which was dark after the glare of the sun. Several ill-perceived figures sat at tables in the shadows. A bald barman leaned on the bar and the place had the odour of tobacco smoke mingled with that of inferior liquor.

Sturgis walked to the bar, feeling the scrutiny of the barman and the shadowed figures.

'I understand I might find Luke Foxton here,' he said to the barman.

The man's eyes widened at the mention of the name and he jerked a finger towards a dark figure sitting in one corner of the room. 'Right there. Big man by the window,' he said tersely.

With his eyes becoming accustomed to the darkness of the interior, Sturgis walked over to the man who occupied a tilted back chair near the window. He wore range garb but his legs, resting on a second chair, bore an expensive pair of tooled leather boots. Sturgis looked at the region of the man's middle. He saw a Navy Colt in a holster tied down to his thigh by a rawhide thong. Luke Foxton wore a black sombrero and his hard eyes glittered in its shadow.

'Luke Foxton?' asked Sturgis.

'Who's asking?' queried Foxton in a languid voice.

'Nate Sturgis.'

'Boss of the Black Eagle mine, over at Vinegar Peak. Folks have heard of you. What do you want – even though folks only ever trouble me for one thing.'

'I can offer you some – er – work,' Sturgis said.

'Then we'll talk money,' Foxton said impassively.

'I heard you sometimes work with Tobe Brant.'

'That can be arranged and it'll cost more money. What's the job?'

'We're troubled at my end of the country by a couple of gunslingers.'

'Names? Do I know 'em?'

'I don't know their names. A pair of skinny guys, one skinnier than the other. They just came out of the blue and they're damned ornery.'

'Don't sound like anyone I know,' said Foxton shaking his head 'And you want their hash settled?'

'Sure thing. I figured the best medicine for a couple of gunslingers is to—'

'Set another couple of specialists against 'em. Specialists is a word I prefer, Mr Sturgis,' stated Foxton, taking his feet off the chair, which he then kicked over to Sturgis by way of offering him a seat. 'So, provided Brant and me do things our way without any interference, let's talk money.'

Half an hour later, Nate Sturgis came out of the saloon, crossed the street and found a fly-blown restaurant where he had an only just palatable meal before climbing into his saddle and taking the desert trail again. A smirk of self satisfaction was on his face.

Back at the W-Bar-F, work on repairing the burned out portion of the headquarters was going steadily ahead and Ghost Canyon was being maintained as an out station of the ranch where the stock was penned. Harry Scott and Pedro Ruiz had rigged up a substantial fence of pickets across the canyon's mouth to prevent straying and the water supply and graze was proving adequate. Scott and Ruiz spent most of the day guarding the animals and bedded down in the canyon at night. At the ranch headquarters, the Flinders brothers, with Walt Harris and Dannehar and Oski, laboured at the repair work.

The sale to Chad Bellingham had a tonic effect on the W-Bar-F. It gave the outfit the feeling that it was still in business and the boost of confidence made Will and Bert Flinders more determined than ever to recover from the raid and to stand their ground in defiance of Nate Sturgis and all Vinegar Peak. There was the added satisfaction of knowing that the Peace Commission's numbers had been reduced by two through the demise of blustering Bull Tuke and one of his companions, although no one deluded himself by imagining that there would not be retaliation from the enemy.

A couple of days passed with activities proceeding with a constant watchfulness and under a tense, ever present awareness that the current situation merely marked a lull in hostilities.

Two nights after the gunplay against Bull Tuke and the Peace Commission riders, two horsemen rode at an unhurried pace through the night on the terrain above the fertile basin in which the W-Bar-F horse ranch lay.

They wore dark clothing and, with one on a black horse and the other on a dun animal, they were almost invisible in the moonless night. Their mounts were burdened with the bedrolls and warsacks of saddle tramps and both riders were lean with impassive expressions. The steady determination of their riding seemed indicative of the steady determination of their intentions.

Foxton and Brant had recently arrived in the Vinegar Peak country and were setting out on their commission.

'Bad medicine' by anyone's standards, the pair were two of the southwest's most dangerous professional killers, who insisted on carrying out their work in their own way which included planning before striking those on whom their 'specialty' was to be practised.

They did not advertise themselves by appearing in townships and making flamboyant displays of themselves in the way of many gunfighters with reputations. Consequently, they avoided Vinegar Peak and made their way to the location of the W-Bar-F by night. Foxton and Brant believed in choosing their killing ground, striking swiftly and, having fulfilled a commission, disappearing from the scene as quickly as possible.

Cephas Dannehar and Slim Oskin, their targets, had become an obsession with Nate Sturgis. The pair had strengthened and spearheaded the brothers' opposition to Black Eagle's plans. He still saw them with blazing Winchesters, stolidly resisting the attackers from Vinegar Peak. He believed that, but for these two strangers, his assault on the ranch might have driven the brothers from the country.

In Skeleton Flat, Sturgis had apprised Luke Foxton of the whereabouts of Dannehar and Oskin so far as he knew them. He presumed they were holed up with the Flinders brothers at the W-Bar-F in which case they would be surrounded by only a handful of men. Sturgis had informed the pair of 'specialists' how things stood in the Vinegar Peak country and how the only law, that of Marshal Tom Cope, was safely in the pocket of the Black Eagle and Peace Commission faction.

Foxton and Brant rode the rim of the basin in which the W-Bar-F lay. They kept their eyes on the dark land below them until they saw a sparse sprinkle of yellow lamplight, indicating a human habitation, clearly the W-Bar-F. They halted when they reached a point almost directly over the ranch buildings and reined up.

'I reckon this spot'll suit us,' said Foxton, 'and there's a stand of oaks yonder where we can bed down.'

They moved away from the rim of the basin, scouted the land and, near the oaks, found a small stream, sufficient to provide drink for their mounts. Then they led their animals to the oaks and unsaddled them. They spread their bedrolls and built a small fire, their position being far enough away from the rim for its flames not to be visible from the ranch below. Coffee was boiled and the two ate a supper of beef jerky and bread, after which they turned in.

Morning came and, at the W-Bar-F, there was early stirring and, with Ruiz and Scott at Ghost Canyon with the stock, the Flinders brothers, Dannehar, Oskin and Walt Harris were hurrying to complete the repair work. They were finishing the restoration of the corrals in strengthening sunlight without knowing, that, from the crest of a slant of land rising beyond the ranch, they were observed by Luke Foxton, lying on his stomach with a spyglass to his eye.

Beside him lay Tobe Brant and the two took good care to keep their heads well down so as to be invisible to the men in the ranch yard.

'Sturgis was right. There's only a handful of them down there,' reported Foxton adjusting the focus of the spyglass. 'And – yeah – I figure I've spotted the two gunnies: both of 'em skinny but one skinnier than the other. Here, take a look.' He passed the telescope to Brant who focussed on the group toiling with corral posts in the yard.

'Shouldn't be too difficult to get at those two,' Brant said. 'Hell, they all look so interested in their work I reckon we could just ride right in there and settle the whole bunch of 'em before they even noticed us.'

Foxton gave a humourless grin. 'We ain't out to get the whole bunch. As usual, I made sure we were paid before doing the job and Sturgis paid only for the two gunsharps. If the other guys horn in, we'll deal with 'em, but it'll be painful to give Sturgis more than he paid for. I don't know who those two are or if they have reputations but before they cash in their chips, I want 'em to know that two better men put them down.'

'You mean you want to challenge 'em?'

'What else? They're gunsharps, same as us and you know damned well that there's what some folks call honour among gunsharps. We're professionals not bushwhackers. We'll go down there and call 'em out and, if those other guys have any horse sense they'll keep out of it and leave the business to the four of us.'

Tobe Brant grinned. 'I always said you were a stickler for formalities,' he said. 'You never did count the dangers but I don't quarrel with you.'

'Never let it be said I forgot that there's honour and dignity in gunfighting, and you can't deny that the dangers are part of the game,' Foxton said.

Ruthless and mercenary, the pair killed without compunction but they subscribed to the curious ethics of those who built reputations by carving notches into their guns. To kill without warning from a concealed position made a man a bushwhacker or a back shooter; to issue a face-to-face challenge and take a gambler's chance on the quickest draw made him a gunfighter. The knife-edge hazards of the game were the same drug as the gambler's belief that Lady Luck might just favour him.

Foxton took the spyglass again and squinted down at the terrain below them.

'I figure we should ride in a wide loop down into the basin, keeping well out of sight of the ranch then swing around to the gate of the yard,' he said at length.

Tobe Brant shrugged. He was always willing to allow Foxton to select the killing ground and the time to strike. He had never yet made a wrong choice and the pair had always escaped the scene with whole skins. Brant had heard that the W-Bar-F crew had put up a furious defence when raided by Sturgis and his followers but the crew were, after all, mere horse wranglers – though the spyglass survey showed that they were carrying sidearms. Once they knew the notorious Foxton and Brant were about their business – and such was Foxton's pride that he would, as usual, announce the fact – they would doubtless be paralysed with fear.

The two walked back to the clump of oaks where their picketed horses were grazing. They saddled up and rode on for a space then descended the sloping land of the basin in a loop well distant from the ranch and its inhabitants, out of whose sight they were kept by various humps and ridges.

On the basin floor, they headed back towards the ranch, then ascended the slant of the land when they saw its buildings above them. They dismounted, slung their reins over their horses' heads so that they hung against their forelegs to prevent the animals from wandering and briefly stretched their legs. Their work was not to be accomplished from the saddle.

Foxton nudged his Navy Colt loose in its leather and Brant did the same with his commonplace but deadly Colt .45. With supreme confidence, they walked forward, overcame a rise in the land and saw the gate of the ranch yard before them.

In the yard, the W-Bar-F men were working on the corrals with their backs to the gate, oblivious to the arrival of the pair, walking soft footedly with only the slightest jingle of spurs.

Foxton and Brant wore expressionless faces which belied their inner surging excitement at, once again, taking a gambler's chance with their lives. They entered the yard, walked several paces forward then some instinct out of Slim Oskin's experience as an army scout caused him to sense danger and he turned suddenly.

He saw the newcomers approaching on foot. From their style, with Foxton's elegantly tooled leather boots and the tied down holsters of both, he knew exactly what they were.

Cephas Dannehar caught his reaction with the corner of his eye and whirled around to see the pair and, as with Oskin, their appearance told him what they were and that they were out to do bloody business on behalf of Nate Sturgis.

Bert Flinders was nearest to Foxton and Brant, lifting a length of peeled pole corral rail. His first glimpse telegraphed to him what this pair were and he knew trouble was imminent.

Foxton and Brant halted and stood together with their right hands dangling close to their holsters.

Foxton called: 'Hey, you two skinny jaspers! You pair of gunslingers! We're Foxton and Brant and we've come—'

Bert Flinders, impulsive as ever, acted swiftly and threw the long corral rail forcefully, sending it flying laterally, directly at the two gunfighters. It smote both across their midriffs and sent them staggering back off their feet.

They landed on their backs and sprawled with the corral rail on top of them. Startled thoughts whirled through their minds. With the precision of men arranging a theatrical presentation, they had planned a different play to be acted out on the ground they had chosen for a speedy killing. An arrogance born of their having usually confronted men scared by their reputations, led them to imagine they could make a slick chore of dispatching the two unknown gunmen. But the W-Bar-F men were not cowering in fear and things were not going according to their scheming.

They scrambled up and their guns were in their hands the instant they tottered to their feet to find Will and Bert Flinders, Dannehar, Oskin and Walt Harris with their weapons already drawn and trained on them.

A tight silence fell between them for an instant and the whole group held frozen poses facing each other, five on one side, two on the other.

The brief impasse was broken by Foxton snarling at Dannehar and Oskin: 'By God, we came to get you two and we'll—'

'Leave them to us,' bawled Dannehar to his companions, seeing the glint of the sun on the mouth of Foxton's pistol, levelled at him.

He fired an instant before Foxton triggered his Colt then dropped to his knees as Foxton's bullet screamed over his head. Foxton fired again but the bullet ploughed into the ground for Foxton was already falling forward stiffly.

The bark of Slim Oskin's pistol followed on the heels of that of Dannehar, Oskin danced aside just as Tobe Brant's gun blasted almost simultaneously with his own, so its bullet missed him by inches. Oskin took no chances with a gunfighter with a known reputation. He fired three times at Brant who could be seen through a haze of blue smoke. Then he was aware of Brant staggering backwards with his mouth wide open.

The W-Bar-F men stood in breathless silence,

looking at the corpse of Foxton lying face down and that of Brant, sprawled on its back. The gunfighters, who had played their hand with professional precision even to observing the twisted chivalry of their calling, had been defeated by the element of surprise.

A wide-eyed Walt Harris turned to Dannehar and Oskin and exclaimed: 'Hell, you beat Foxton and Brant!'

'Thanks to Bert,' Dannehar said. 'In another split second, they'd have drawn fast and made cold meat of Slim and me, but for Bert throwing that pole. They seemed to have the strange notion that we're a pair of gunslingers with reputations.'

'You are now,' said Bert Flinders gravely. 'You're the pair who shot Luke Foxton and Tobe Brant. That's some reputation to be branded with.'

CHAPTER NINE

A DELIVERY FOR STURGIS

Will Flinders gazed at the two corpses. 'I figured Sturgis would make another move sooner or later but I never reckoned on Foxton and Brant showing up,' he said, 'so we're stuck with having to dispose of the bodies of two notorious *hombres*.'

The whole W-Bar-F crew, including Harry Scott and Pedro Ruiz who had hastened down to the ranch from Ghost Canyon when they heard shooting, were standing around the ranch's buck-board which now bore the bodies of Foxton and Brant. The gunfighters' horses had been retrieved from where they were left and were now drinking at the trough.

'Take 'em back to Sturgis,' said old Harry Scott flatly. 'If he paid for 'em, let him have 'em.'

This brought a whoop of delight from Bert Flinders. It was a notion that suited his reckless spirit.

'How should we do that?' asked Oskin.

'Easily enough,' Scott said. 'We can take 'em into town on the buck-board with the whole kaboodle of us escorting 'em with plenty of armaments and we'll deliver 'em to the Black Eagle offices just as if we were the United States Post Office.'

The usually cautious Will Flinders grinned. The idea had a piquancy that stirred even his usually grave demeanour. 'I like the sound of it, Harry, but the whole town is against us and we'd be outnumbered if it came to gunplay.'

'I say we do it,' enthused Bert Flinders. 'I've been itching to take a rise out of that damned town all along.'

'We know all about that and we pulled you out of hot water once already. You were plumb harebrained,' said his brother. 'The whole bunch of us, well armed, might get away with it, though. I sure don't see why Foxton and Brant should be buried on W-Bar-F land.'

'We'll need eyes in the back of our heads in case someone wants to throw lead,' said Cephas Dannehar. 'But I reckon it would be a real eloquent gesture to dump Foxton and Brant on Sturgis.'

'Let's take the chance,' said Slim Oskin. And the whole gathering grinned at each other in agreement.

It had just turned noon when the party of W-Bar-F riders, escorting the ranch's buck-board, entered the street of Vinegar Peak.

The two Flinders sat at the front of the wagon, Will handling the reins and Bert with a Winchester carbine slanted across his middle. The rest of the W-Bar-F crew rode alongside them and the wagon contained the corpses of Foxton and Brant. Tethered behind the vehicle were the saddled horses of the two hired gunmen, laden with their trail gear.

They came into Vinegar Peak's street like a solemn procession, with every man keeping a sharp eyed watch on either side of the street and the curious knots of townsfolk beginning to gather.

The W-Bar-F men were now in the nest of the rattlesnakes but, so far, no one was offering any hostility though, only nights before, almost the entire population of this town had waged furious war against the W-Bar-F. The town might yet blow up in their faces like a powder keg.

Reckless Bert Flinders was enjoying the situation. It was satisfying his desire to make a defiant gesture against Nate Sturgis and his faction, and no greater insult could be offered than to return the bodies of the paid, big reputation assassins as proof that the W-Bar-F was still alive and fighting.

The offices of the Black Eagle company occupied a tall clapboard building fronting the street, and behind it bulked a rising shoulder of sandy coloured land, topped by the surface rig of the mine.

There was a stretch of plankwalk in front of the building and the party from the horse ranch stopped in front of it.

A growing crowd of the curious had followed the buck-board and party along the street and they stood around, watching. Bert Flinders stood in the forepart of the wagon, his carbine at the ready, with his brother beside him with a levelled revolver. Dannehar and Oskin dismounted and stood facing the frontage of the offices with drawn six-guns.

A murmur ran through the crowd as Walt Harris and Pedro Ruiz, between them, took hold of Luke Foxton's body, slid it off the wagon and carried it to the front of the office. They laid it out on the plank sidewalk, walked purposefully back to the buck-board, took the corpse of Tobe Brant and laid it out beside that of Foxton.

Dannehar and Oskin covered the front of the office and the remainder of the party, with ready trigger fingers, kept a sharp watch on the crowd.

Still no hostility was shown by the Vinegar Peak citizenry.

Harris and Ruiz took the gunfighters' laden horses from the rear of the wagon, led them to the hitch rack outside the offices of the mine and tethered them.

In an upper room of the building, Nate Sturgis was in conversation with two of the Kansas City based directors of the company who had arrived without warning on that morning's stage. Heavily bearded and clad in city suits, they had fat cigars slanting from their whisker fringed mouths and both frequently scowled.

The usually city bound directors had bestirred themselves to journey into Arizona Territory because disturbing rumours had reached them. It seemed that Nate Sturgis, who had already established a reputation for heavy-handedness, was carrying on a form of private war. President of the mining company he might be, but there were directors and shareholders, men of stolid respectability – some of them Quakers – were all for peace. They wanted nothing of the bullet-bitten methods of the western frontier and the Black Eagle hierarchy was not pleased with Sturgis.

The visiting city men had just acquainted Sturgis with their fears for the good name of the Black Eagle company and Sturgis was answering them heatedly.

'Gentlemen,' he growled, 'the Boss of Vinegar Peak they call me, and with good reason. I'm a company president who believes in working at the heart of things. That's why I prefer to be right here at the base of operations and soft handed ways don't work here. I made the mine the centre of affairs in this town. Damn it, not only do the miners get a living by it, tradesman and storekeepers prosper because the mine is here.'

He puffed out his chest like a pigeon and said piously: 'I even formed the Peace Commission, a body of reliable men who ensure the community is kept safe from wrongdoers. They are supported by the businessmen, the saloonkeepers and traders. I plan to make the company even stronger but there are those who want to hang on to their land and their old ideas in the face of progress. They just can't see that the way ahead in these new territories is to have big and efficient business—'

Sturgis was all set to launch himself into one of his windy speeches when a hubbub from the street below penetrated the room by way of an open window and cut him short.

Walking to the window, he looked down into the street, saw the buckboard and the crowd and caught his breath at the sight of the party from the W-Bar-F with their drawn weapons. Then his jaw dropped on seeing the two corpses laid out almost reverently.

'Hell,' he hissed into his beard, 'Foxton and Brant dead, and the Flinders bunch and those two damned, skinny gunsharps have had the nerve to bring them into town!' He swept back one side of his broadcloth frock coat and slapped his hand on the butt of the Colt .45 holstered at his hip.

With a face as black as thunder, he turned to the men from Kansas City. 'Excuse me, gentlemen,' he barked. 'I'm required downstairs.' And he strode out of the room.

Downstairs, he shoved two goggling clerks away from the window of the front door, hauled the door open and stepped out. In the garish sunlight, the two corpses lay almost at his feet and the guns of Dannehar and Oskin were levelled directly at him.

Sturgis stood in the doorway, glowering at the party from the W-Bar-F and the crowd which had swelled considerably. It was taking some time for him to absorb the fact that his hired trigger men had failed in their mission and were now stretched in death on his doorstep. His hand was on the butt of his holstered gun but stilled by the menace of the firearms of Dannehar and Oskin.

The crowd shifted and some fell back hastily from the vicinity of the buck-board as Sturgis quivered with fury and twitched his gun hand, as if about to draw.

Bert Flinders gave a derisive hoot. 'Don't risk it,

Sturgis,' he called cheerfully. 'You wouldn't want to mix it with the two who gave Foxton and Brant their comeuppance. And, remember, there's a city ordinance against shooting on the street. You might find yourself arrested by Marshal Cope.'

Sturgis stared in impotent rage at the intruders who, at the very moment important company visitors were in town, had boldly entered the domain where he ruled the roost and flung this insult in his face. It was then that three range-garbed, gun-heavy men came down the street, riders of the Peace Commission, a force now depleted after the demise of Bull Tuke and Billy Twist and the defections of Marsh and O'Phelim.

The Peace Commission men, attracted by the incident and the display of weapons outside the Black Eagle offices, drifted towards it but Cephas Dannehar swung his Colt towards them. The three, seeing the bodies of Foxton and Brant for the first time, halted and looked about them bewilderedly.

'Stand still and don't think of trying anything,' warned Dannehar.

The three froze in the face of the many weapons pointing at them and Sturgis stood with his brain spinning under the impact of the events of the last few minutes. His two hirelings, with reputations as deadly assassins, had been killed and brought brazenly into town by what amounted to an invasion force of his enemies. A goodly number of the citizenry who had followed his aggressive lead only nights before now stood around dumb and open mouthed and his private force of ruffians were nowhere to be seen when the W-Bar-F men arrived. Into the bargain, he was all too aware that the influential Black Eagle men from Kansas City were probably at the upstairs window, witnessing the humiliation and rage of the man who claimed to rule Vinegar Peak.

He found his voice at last and loosed his fury at the crowd, roaring harshly: 'Well, are you all going to stand around like dummies and let this bunch ride in here and do just as they please? Enough of you are armed. Why don't you drive them out?' But his own hand still remained, as if frozen, on the butt of his revolver and the cluster of townsfolk did not stir.

A mocking voice called out of their midst: 'Nothing doing, Sturgis. Maybe the town followed you to the W-Bar-F to raise hell but human beings are fickle and a tolerable number have lost their stomach for shooting scrapes.'

Sturgis knew that voice well. It was that of the blacksmith, Wally Drever, who had always been hostile to Sturgis and his methods.

'Sure. A lot of folk figure one battle is one too many,' shouted another voice, that of Jim Simms, backing up his crony, Drever.

A collective grumble rippled through the crowd and Sturgis felt a cold wave skewer through his innards. This vocal dissent was a symbol of something he had sensed in the last couple of days – the feeling of a falling away of the support of the townsfolk. It was of a piece with the defections of Marsh and O'Phelim.

Sturgis quivered with pent-up rage. Now, more than ever, he was aware that his grip on Vinegar Peak was slipping. He was acutely aware, too, that he had been all too publicly forced into a corner by the W-Bar-F men and made to appear helpless.

Up on the buck-board, Will Flinders gestured with his firearm to the corpses lying on the plank sidewalk. 'Better do the decent thing by your two late friends and convey them to the undertaker, Sturgis,' he called. 'And you can buckle down to the idea that the W-Bar-F is still alive and kicking and in business.'

'Yeah, and doing so well we've opened another branch out as far as Ghost Canyon,' shouted his mischievous brother.

A tense silence fell on the crowd in the street and on Sturgis and his Peace Commission riders, as Will Flinders holstered his six-gun and took up the reins again. He flicked the reins and, as he turned the buck-board about, his brother remained standing with his Winchester trained on Sturgis and his three companions in front of the offices.

114

Dannehar, Oskin, Harris, Ruiz and Scott remounted and sat turned about in their saddles with six-guns pointed as the party moved off along the street. Sturgis and his henchmen and the citizenry still showed no reaction.

Inwardly, Nate Sturgis cursed his luck. In a matter of hours, everything seemed to have worked against him. His stormy spirit goaded him to shoot at the W-Bar-F party, outgunned though he was, but his belligerence was curbed by the presence of the influential Black Eagle directors. He dared not turn to look up at the window of the upper office but he knew the pair must have seen everything that had passed on the street below.

In a turmoil of brooding anger, he watched the buck-board and riders raise the dust of the street as they progressed back to the W-Bar-F. Then he signalled to the Peace Commission men to convey the two dead men to the undertaker's premises across the street.

He could feel the mocking quality of the gaze of the disaffected crowd as he turned and strode back into the building. Upstairs, covering his deflated spirits, he took the initiative at once and presented his version of events to the directors: 'I presume you saw what went on out there. Two men in my employ were murdered and the ruffians responsible brought their bodies into town.'

'That crowd of people seemed angry with you,'

said one of the visitors.

'Naturally,' Sturgis blustered. 'They're always angry when things occasionally go wrong, in spite of my efforts to preserve law and order. But they know justice will be done in the end. Marshal Tom Cope is a good lawman and the Peace Commission unit is intelligent and active. We'll overcome those ruffians in our own time and in our own way. You've just sampled the facts of life in a raw mining town. You can tell the head office that this is not Kansas City and hard remedies are needed here. If I'm accused of being heavy-handed it's because I know the ugly moods of this country. I know the remedies for trouble and I know what I'm doing.'

The directors considered him with hard eyes under frowning brows and both appeared markedly unconvinced. Sturgis had the uneasy feeling that, watching from the window, they were not impressed by his performance when facing the crowd. In that, he was correct. The dumping of two corpses at his feet by a group of armed men who simply rode away afterwards gave a decided hollowness to his boasts of both the Vinegar Peak Peace Commission as a force for law and order, and the efficiency of Marshal Tom Cope, who never made an appearance throughout the incident.

One visitor remained silent and lit another cigar while keeping a steady, disdainful gaze on Sturgis.

The other said firmly: 'We will not delay much longer. We understand there is a late stage back to the railhead this evening. We'll be taking it.'

CHAPTER TEN

CHAOS IN THE CANYON

Nate Sturgis sat at his desk in his lamplit office in a darkly brooding mood. It was night and, a few hours before, the visiting directors from Kansas city had departed on the late stage.

Sturgis fumed with anger after the men from the W-Bar-F brought the corpses of Foxton and Brant to Vinegar Peak. It fuelled his obsession with the Flinders brothers and, particularly, with Dannehar and Oskin who, he had no doubt, had been the cause of their deaths. If the pair had dispatched the two high-reputation gunfighters, it spoke of the quality of their gun savvy but Sturgis, in his near mad vengeful mood, was unfazed by

118

them. In fact, his obsession had almost tipped him over the edge of logical thought.

No matter how dangerously skilled the gunmen aiding the brothers were, he wanted revenge for every misfortune of recent days that had brought about the disturbing sensation that he was rapidly losing his grasp as kingpin of Vinegar Peak.

He wanted to strike another blow against the Flinders brothers and their faction out of pure hatred, for he had almost lost sight of the original objective of acquiring their land for the expansion of the Black Eagle holdings, From its origins as a matter of business, his opposition to them had now become a personal vendetta.

The name of Ghost Canyon kept recurring in his brain. He could hear Bert Flinders's mocking voice calling from the buck-board, saying something about the W-Bar-F having a 'branch' at Ghost Canyon. What did that mean?

He rose from his desk and crossed to a table which held an assortment of papers. He then picked up a large folded map, carried it to his desk and unfolded it. It was a chart of Arizona Territory, as surveyed by the US Army a few years before.

Sturgis carefully spread it on his desk and adjusted the lamplight so he could see its outlines more clearly. He studied the Vinegar Peak region, found the location where the W-Bar-F ranch now stood then found Ghost Canyon, marked some distance away on public land, adjoining that now owned by the W-bar-F. The army surveyors had marked its pueblo of ancient tribal dwellings as a ruin.

What could horse ranchers want with a place like Ghost Canyon? Then he spotted the creek running through the canyon. The region was not described as desert and the presence of the creek suggested graze. Sturgis gave a sardonic laugh of triumph. The Flinders's outfit must have stock at the canyon even though it was not part of their land.

The location was a considerable distance from the W-Bar-F headquarters and, if stock grazed there, it might be vulnerable.

Then he spotted something else. A jagged line less than a mile from the rear exit of the canyon was labelled as a deep arroyo, a dried up water-course, of an estimated two hundred feet deep. Sturgis studied it and tugged at his beard thought-fully. He began to form a plan. That there was W-Bar-F stock at Ghost Canyon was only conjec-tured from Bert Flinders's parting remark but, if there was, he saw a way of striking a hard blow at the brothers. This time, it would be done without any aid from the citizens of Vinegar Peak whom he now regarded as fickle and lily-livered.

He made a mental count of the number of Peace Commission riders left after the recent losses. It came to nine.

Next, he looked to his weapons, cleaning and fully loading his revolver and carbine. Then he turned in. It had hardly been the best day of his life but he swore he would make the next night wholly satisfying.

The following morning, he sent word around the remaining Peace Commission men to gather at his office. He looked at their hard and anything but attractive countenance, hoping he would not see any signs of the disillusion that caused Marsh and O'Phelim to desert.

'We've had two killed and two more quit,' he stated flatly. 'If any of you have lost your guts for action, say so now and you'll be paid off. Otherwise, we have work on hand to settle the hash of those damned horse farmers. And it'll be done tonight.'

Shorty Sleeman, a small but dangerous border drifter, said to be wanted in Mexico for murder, ceased chewing his plug of tobacco and spoke up.

'Ain't no quitters here as long as you're paying good wages, Mr Sturgis', he said, and there was a general rumble of agreement.

Sturgis thought that, at least, this bulk of the Peace Commission's force had not been contaminated by the desire to abandon his bellicose plans for the betterment of the Black Eagle company and, as he had always insisted, the furtherance of

Vinegar Peak township. Encouraged, he spread out the map on his desk and the party of riders gathered around it.

That same day, there was a relaxed and jubilant atmosphere at the W-Bar-F Ranch after the happenings at Vinegar Peak. The crew had the feeling that they had drawn the teeth of Sturgis and his faction, and the passive behaviour of the crowd indicated that Vinegar Peak was no longer ready to jump to his commands.

Work on repairing the damage caused by the raid was almost totally completed, the corrals had been repaired and were again fit to hold numerous animals, separated into stallions, mares and colts.

Harry Scott and Pedro Ruiz were still wrangling the stock kept at Ghost Canyon but it was decided to bring the animals back from there to the home grazing grounds the next day. With the first shades of evening, Scott glanced at the sky. It promised a clear, balmy night, a prospect that suited Scott and Ruiz for it would be their last night of sleeping under the stars. The following morning, they, with the rest of the crew, would drive the herd of horse-flesh back to the W-Bar-F pastures and corrals.

A couple of hours later, the two settled down in their established camping place, under the canyon wall which held the crumbling, climbing pueblo of ancient dwellings, lit their fire and began to rustle up supper.

A couple of hours after darkness had fallen, with a wafer of a moon silvering the landscape, the pair spread their bedrolls and turned in.

Towards midnight, a company of intruders approached the opening to Ghost Canyon. They had travelled by a circuitous route, avoiding the W-Bar-F, and they rode in twos with Nate Sturgis in the lead.

He and the residue of Peace Commission force walked th elast portion of their journey, leading their horses to make as little noise as possible, since they suspected the W-Bar-F would have posted a guard at the canyon if there truely were horses there. They moved cautiously, with the jingling of horse trappings kept to a minimum. At their head, Sturgis had his mind on vicious revenge against the Flinders brothers and, with a smirk of satisfaction, he heard the whinney of a horse from within the canyon. It sounded as if this venture would not be in vain.

The intruders reached the picket fence, spread across the canyon's entrance to hold back strays. Working by the slight light of the moon, they discovered that it could be drawn back to allow passage in and out of the canyon and, with it partially opened, they led their horses stealthily in and mounted up silently.

Finding the course of the creek, they followed it and, from up ahead, heard occasional snorts and the shifting of hoofs, indicating a number of horses.

Bedded down near the old Indian ruins, Harry Scott was disturbed. He opened his eyes and listened. A snuffling and sporadic whinnying came from the direction of the creek in the depths of the canyon. The experience of his years as a horse wrangler told Scott that something was amiss with the herd. He listened again, heard the tell-tale sounds again, reasoned that a coyote might have found its way to the herd then he heard the faint but unmistakable clink of a saddle horse's ring bit.

He scrambled out of his bedroll, got to his knees, fumbled for his boots and clothing, put them on hastily, then grabbed his shellbelt and holstered six-gun, lying at his side, and buckled it on. With his foot, he nudged Ruiz in the bedroll beside him.

'Somebody's out yonder. Somebody on a horse,' he whispered.

Pedro Ruiz became fully awake at once, pounced on his clothing and found his handgun. Both men stared into the canyon. Its high walls allowed only limited moonlight to penetrate far into its depths but the two discerned shadowy movements close to the creek, some distance away. There was an evident shifting of a number of animals with attendant urgings in low voices where wranglers would normally use lusty whoopings and

vigorous flapping of the arms to move the crea-
tures.

'Damn! Someone's rustling the stock! There's a
whole bunch of 'em by the sound of it,' said Ruiz,
keeping his voice low. He secured his Colt around
his waist and, like Scott, grabbed his Winchester.

The pair moved quickly but quietly, running
under the shadow of the rearing canyon wall
towards the sound of the activity.

They halted, listened again and the sounds were
now more distinct. Scott tapped Ruiz on the shoulder and, in the dim light, indicated the set of old
Indian dwellings piled one on top of the other and
rising up the wall of the canyon behind them.

'We can spot them from up there and fire from
a high position if it comes to shooting,' he whispered.

Together, keeping low, they ran along the
canyon wall and found the beginning of the
upward climbing zigzag path leading to the
dwellings that were, in fact, caves fronted by
ancient adobe facings. The pathway was narrow
and there was danger of their slipping over the
edge, but they persisted in running upward as fast
as they could. Just as the pair took cover in one of
the dwellings high on the rocky wall, the fickle
moon emerged from behind a cloud and shed a
better than usual light on the bed of the canyon.

Scott and Ruiz looked down from behind a

weather worn adobe wall and saw several riders herding the collection of horses crowded around the creek. They seemed intent on driving the animals back through the canyon toward its rear. The horses, having had several days of free grazing, were reluctant to respond. Some were not responding all, but shying away from the riders, so they had to be chased individually.

The moonlight gave a sudden glimpse of one rider's darkly bearded face as he swerved his mount in pursuit of a spirited colt.

'Sturgis!' gasped Ruiz. 'It's Sturgis and his gang! They got past us while we slept! Why are they trying to drive the stock out through the back of the canyon?'

Scott searched his brain, raking over what he knew of the country beyond the rear of the canyon, which was mostly wasteland on the fringe of the desert. Then he remembered the arroyo with its treacherous steep sides and the long drop to its rocky, arid bed.

'Hell, there's nothing out that way except waste-land and a deep arroyo!' he whispered urgently. The significance of the arroyo hit him. 'It looks like they're out to drive the stock over the edge of the gully. Every one of them will be killed! That'll ruin the outfit.'

'Damn it, what can we do to stop them from up here?' Ruiz said. He shifted his position behind the adobe structure, but in doing so he raised his Winchester a little above the wall.

At that moment, the moon touched a brief silver sheen to the weapon.

Down on the floor of the canyon, in the midst of the restless animals, one of the horsemen gave a yelp, hauled his six-gun from leather, and fired at the wall of the canyon.

The bullet bounced off the rock face near Pedro Ruiz's head with an echoing whine. The herd of horses reacted by rearing, surging and spinning in near panic.

In a towering rage, Sturgis peered through the gloom and swerved his mount through the spooked animals in the direction of the man who fired. He came alongside him and growled savagely: 'What the hell is wrong with you? Why did you fire?'

'I saw a movement in the old Indian houses up yonder. Figured I saw someone up there,' gabbled the man.

'So you fired and scared all the cayuses. It's hard enough to control them as it is,' snorted Sturgis. 'There's nobody up there. Are you scared by the old stories about ghosts in this place, you fool?'

'I reckon there is someone up there. I saw the moonlight shine on something, maybe a gun,' persisted the man.

Another rider steered his fractious horse

through the mass of restless animals and reached Sturgis. 'I figure there is someone there, Mr Sturgis,' he said breathlessly. 'I think I caught sight of a movement just a few moments ago. You never know what goes on in this place. It's damned creepy.'

'Blast it!' exploded Sturgis. 'Have I got a bunch of half-wits, scared of shadows, on my hands? Put your minds to calming these horses and driving them through the canyon and forget about what you imagine you saw. And no more shooting.'

But the single shot loosed by the scared Peace Commission man was having an effect. Its thinned down report was carried on the still night air across the grazing grounds of the W-Bar-F to the ranch headquarters.

In the ranch house, Bert Flinders, in whom a habit of sleeping lightly had been induced by the recent disturbances, heard it and was jerked out of his slumber. He listened for any further shooting, heard none, but was sufficiently satisfied that he had truly heard the report and that it came from the direction of Ghost Canyon. He leapt out of bed, rushed from his room and flung open the door of his brother's room next to his own.

'Wake up, Will! There's shooting at the canyon!' he called. He charged into the room and shook his brother, who was drowsily surfacing from sleep.

'You've been dreaming,' mumbled Will, reluctant to leave his bed.

'Dreaming nothing,' persisted Bert urgently. 'I heard a shot from that direction. Something's going on out that way and the whole of our stock is there. Hell, we don't want to lose even a hair off one of those horses!'

This prompted Will to tumble out of bed and Bert hared out of the house, unclothed though he was, to run across the yard and alarm the men in the bunkhouse.

Back at Ghost Canyon, Harry Scott and Pedro Ruiz held their positions in the old pueblo, keeping under cover. Their high position might have given them an advantage in picking off the raiders, but for the darkness of the night and the confusion of the dimly seen, restless, swirling tide of horses below. The animals were still jittery and unmanageable through the scared rider's reckless shot. For the time being, the intruders were thwarted in their plan to move the animals back through the canyon.

There was a flurry of activity at the W-Bar-F with the Flinders brothers, Dannehar and Oskin and Walt Harris, hastily dressing, grabbing weapons and dashing to the stables to rig their horses. Within ten minutes of leaving their blankets, they were pounding over the dark landscape, splitting the wind for Ghost Canyon.

Raking their mounts with spurs, they left the

W-Bar-F holdings behind and traversed the tangled public land with its distant rise of mesas and wind sculptured rock formations.

They reached the opening of the canyon, where the picket fencing had been pulled aside, raced in and passed the camp site of Scott and Ruiz with its abandoned bedrolls, almost dead fire and two picketed horses. From the depths of the canyon, they heard a hubbub of snorts and trampling hoofs and charged towards it.

Now, the first long, gold and silver streaks of dawn were beginning to spread over the sky, bringing a cold, sharp light to the inner canyon. Ahead of them, the W-Bar-F men saw the herd of horses, moving in a sluggish and uncertain way, heading for the rear of the canyon with several riders urging them forward.

One, flourishing a six-gun, turned his saddle at the sound of the newly arrived horsemen. The dawn light showed him to be a familiar Peace Commission rider who levelled his weapon at the oncoming intruders. The sight of him identified the group herding the horses.

'Sturgis and his gang!' shouted Dannehar, ducking his head down to the horn of his saddle.

Then the blast of a powerful shot clattered through the canyon and the man stiffened upright and lurched backwards, falling from his mount, shot through the head. A curl of gunsmoke drifted off the face of the dwellings up on the canyon's side.

A head in a familiar Mexican sugarloaf hat made a brief appearance over the low adobe wall outside one of the ancient dwellings and the voice of Pedro Ruiz called: 'They're aiming to drive the horses over the edge of the arroyo behind the canyon!' He disappeared just as he was spotted by a Sturgis horseman who loosed an ineffective shot in his direction.

The arrival of the men from the W-Bar-F, and the shot, caused some of the order in the horses to unravel. They began milling and jumping nervously, but Sturgis and his men continued to herd them on through the canyon, though progress slowed.

The W-Bar-F men drew closer and a further couple of shots from up in the Indian structures dropped another pair of the herders from their saddles. Now, Harry Scott was seen in the high pueblo and Ruiz was glimpsed in a totally different place from before, both were wielding smoking Winchesters. Almost immediately, they disappeared again.

The two had found an interesting aspect to the long abandoned dwellings. Arranged in rows and climbing the canyon wall, one tier upon another, each small habitation was long unexplored. The interiors, blackened by the cooking fires of centuries, were now the haunts of gila monsters, rock lizards and serpents and Scott and Ruiz had discovered that, laterally, each was connected to its next door neighbours on either side by way of a narrow passage at the rear.

The passages were probably a means of keeping individual groups from becoming bottled up in one dwelling in time of tribal war, and they permitted Scott and Ruiz to fire from outside one small cave-house, swiftly disappear inside it and use the passages to emerge from another dwelling. The strengthening light of day allowed them to pick off riders from their high vantage point.

Down in the canyon, there was a frenzied mêlée of men and horses. Some of the animals were now running in panic at full stretch for the rear of the canyon and would quickly be on the open flat, heading directly for the arroyo. Soon the whole herd would be following them and, if not stopped, they would be pitching over the edge of the gully like lemmings.

Cephas Dannehar, crouching low, saw the danger and, in the mass of swirling horseflesh and men, he glimpsed Oskin, riding close to him.

'Head up front, Slim!' he bellowed. 'We've got to drive 'em back.'

The peril of the situation had already communicated itself to Oskin, who was trying to keep out of the crossfire put up by Sturgis and his men.

Scott and Ruiz were making a nuisance of themselves, appearing and vanishing at various points of the canyon wall dwellings, and blasting away with their Winchesters. Oskin waved to his W-Bar-F colleagues, indicating what clear space there was ahead of them and they followed him, forcing their animals to join Dannehar up near the head of the runaways.

In the midst of the surging horses almost filling the whole width of the canyon floor, Sturgis and his crew were too preoccupied with the sniping of Ruiz and Scott to notice that the whole company of W-Bar-F men had managed to detach themselves from the mêlée. They had forced their mounts through the scant free space to the head of the running animals, now close to the rear outlet of the canyon.

The uneven ground, scattered with boulders, cactus and catclaw, made for uneven going and, when the men from the horse ranch – with Dannehar and Oskin in the lead – reached the end of the canyon, they realized that a number of horses had already escaped and were pounding at growing speed towards the arroyo only a mile away. Others were streaming after them in a frenzied panic to get clear of the shooting, echoing from wall to wall of the canyon.

It was full morning now, with the sun well over the horizon. Plumes of dry dust were raised by a myriad of thundering hoofs and, partially blinded by it, Dannehar and Oskin, with the Flinders brothers and Walt Harris close behind, raced alongside the herd on its right side. Their hope was to outrun the horses, before they reached the drop into the arroyo, wheel in front of them and scare them into turning and running back the way they came.

Such was the speed of the frightened gathering of animals, that it seemed an eternity before the riders made any headway towards outstripping them. Urging, spurring and spitting dust, they were aware that they were eating up the distance and the lip of the arroyo could not be far ahead.

Abruptly, Dannehar and Oskin realized that they were getting ahead of the leading runaways and Bert Flinders was hard on their heels. All three strove to force more effort out of their mounts and slowly drew ahead of the horse herd. They took off their hats and began to wave at them, whooping and yelling with dry throats and gradually drawing in front of the herd, wheeling almost in its path.

A couple of leading horses, slithered, reared and shied away from the distraction of the yelling and gesticulating riders then made a complete left turn, causing the rest to follow their lead and run back. The W-Bar-F men pranced their horses in front of what became a wheeling tide of horseflesh turning back on itself. Their speed slackened and

Dannehar, Oskin and Bert Flinders, joined by his brother, halted in front of the animals and continued to whoop at them to keep them moving back to almost clog the rear outlet of Ghost Canyon.

They put in a strenuous ten minutes of hoarse yelling, charging and wheeling their mounts through banners of dust to clear scared horses from the stretch of land between the outlet of the canyon and the edge of the arroyo.

As the animals ran back into the canyon and the immediate danger subsided, Will FLinders happened to squint through the swirling fog of risen dust and gave a startled cry: 'Hey! Do you realize where we are? Take care!'

Dannehar, Oskin, Bert Flinders and Walt Harris looked around, piercing the obscuring dust with slitted eyes, and realized that, in tackling the undisciplined horse herd, all had backed so near to the wide arroyo as to almost on its edge.

Slim Oskin was nearest to the dizzying drop with his horse's hoofs almost on the lip and Will Flinders's warning yell came too late for him. Surprised, he looked down into the void and his horse did the same. The animal took fright, gave a quivering whinney and reared, taking a jump to get clear of the danger.

Oskin was totally unprepared for its action. He lurched in the saddle, his boots slithered out of his stirrups and he was thrown backwards, unseated, to disappear from view over the edge of the deep chasm.

CHAPTER ELEVEN

A PLAN FOR
SUDDEN DEATH

In Ghost Canyon, Ruiz and Scott were harassing Sturgis and his riders by firing down at them from their elevated position, using the dwellings and their connecting passages to rapidly appear and disappear at different points. They fired quickly and accurately and dispatched four of the Peace Commission men who tried to fight back from the midst of surging and milling horses, alarmed by the crashing gunfire echoing from wall to wall of the canyon. The jostling of the disturbed animals meant that the Peace Commission men scarcely ever loosed a bullet with any accuracy.

For Ruiz and Scott, their exploits in the Indian

pueblo and the precision of their sniping with Winchesters had taught them something about each other. They came together in one of the dwellings and Pedro Ruiz said admiringly: 'This is not the first time you've done this kind of work, Harry, where did you learn to fire like that?'

'Defending Fredericksburg against the Yankees in the big war, using an old time Springfield musket,' answered Scott. 'You're not so bad yourself. Where did you learn this trade?'

Ruiz gave a sly chuckle. 'Let's say it's a skill I picked up,' he said.

Scott grinned and pumped another round into his carbine. 'I always knew you had a murky past. I figured you were one of those blamed Mexican border raiders.'

Ruiz chuckled again and said piously: 'If I was, I'm reformed now.'

Their vantage point gave them a view of a sudden change in the behaviour of the horses on the canyon floor. Their shifting and milling became more agitated and their numbers appeared to be increasing. This was because the animals that had been shooed back into the rear exit of the canyon by Dannehar, Oskin, Harris and the Flinders brothers were now well inside, and moving towards the opening at the further end, forcing the animals already in the canyon to wheel around and travel in the same direction as the newly entered ones.

Scott and Ruiz glimpsed Sturgis and what remained of his Peace Commission henchmen, scattered in the midst of the animals and fighting to remain on horseback as their mounts were carried along by the equestrian tide. Then the pair in the old pueblo realized that their enemies were striving to escape from the canyon by heading for the way they had entered.

'Looks like they're licked and hightailing,' grinned Harry Scott to himself as he fired a random shot to set the echoes ringing and hasten Sturgis and his companions on their way.

At the scene of Slim Oskin's disappearance into the arroyo, Cephas Dannehar was the first to dismount, reach the edge and look into the chasm. The sides of the arroyo were not sheer. They were steeply slanting inclines of loose shale and stony scree, broken by scattered outcrops of huge, red, weather-worn rocks like buttresses.

Dannehar could see nothing of Oskin. He did not appear to be on the downward slope below the lip nor could he be seen on the bed far below.

Dannehar lowered himself over the rim of the chasm and began a cautious descent. He slithered feet first down the slant of loose shale and scattered rocks, raising a harsh dust. The going was difficult and he could only control the speed of his descent by digging his heels deep into the shifting surface of the slope. He went down fifteen or twenty yards in a sometimes halting and sometimes involuntary quickened sliding, but could see no sign of Oskin.

Then, a good distance below him, he caught sight of an overhanging outcrop of rock from under which a boot protruded. He moved crab-wise across the uncertain surface to slide down nearer to the rock.

He found Oskin, lying under the outcrop, slanted across the shale and scree, possibly unconscious but perhaps dead. Dannehar put on a spurt, trying to regulate his progress until he reached the rock. He dug his heels in hard to halt beside Oskin.

There was a patch of blood around the ribs on Oskin's left side and a bloody bruise on his forehead. His hat was missing, but his six-gun was still in its holster. He was covered in ochre dusk, but he was breathing.

Dannehar grasped his shoulders and hauled him from under the outcrop with difficulty. He manoeuvred himself above Oskin, rolled on his back and, with legs apart, reached between them to grip Oskin's shoulders. He began a slow progress on his back, moving upward by shoving his legs, pulling Oskin behind him. He panted heavily with the effort and the thick dust got into his throat and nose, causing him to spit and snort.

At times, he seemed to be moving by inches, breathing labouredly and frequently stopping to catch his breath. There was a constant danger that the two of them would go into an uncontrolled slide all the way down the side of the declivity to the rocky, cactus tangled bed of the old water-course. Perspiring and grunting, Dannehar made his slow and laborious way up the slant, hauling Oskin's weight in a series of jerks.

Suddenly, a length of lariat came snaking out of the air and landed beside him. He heard Bert Flinders yelling from above: 'Here, Cephas! Tie it around his shoulders.'

Dannehar twisted his head to look upward. He saw his companions peering over the upper rim where they held the other end of the lariat. He croaked an acknowledgement and tied the rope in a loop under the unconscious man's arms and across his chest.

He waved a signal to the men above him and they began to haul Oskin up.

Dannehar scrambled up beside him, easing Oskin's progress as much as he could. Eventually, the two reached the top of the incline and were grasped by the brothers and Harris and lifted over the arroyo's edge. Dannehar now found that the last of the horse herd had been driven into the canyon and only the saddle horses of the W-Bar-F men were in evidence.

141

The W-Bar-F men examined Oskin, concluding that he struck his head and became unconscious when he fell into the arroyo. Bert Flinders brought his canteen from his saddle gear and splashed water in Oskin's face, who slowly came to and looked around dazedly as he was given the canteen to drink from.

'I reckon I'm mostly all right, but for a hell of an ache in my ribs,' he gasped in reply to his companions' questions as to how he felt.

Dannehar opened Oskin's blood stained shirt and concluded that the blood resulted from lacerations received when he slid down the ragged surface of the arroyo's side. Oskin winced when Dannehar ran his hands over his ribs and his breathing was irregular.

'Something's wrong,' announced Dannehar, frowning. 'I figure you could have broken some ribs. Maybe you need a doctor.'

'No,' Oskin objected scornfully. 'I'll be good as new in an hour or two. I've suffered a damned sight worse in my time. There's no call for a doctor.'

Dannehar and the others were not convinced and, as they assisted him into his saddle, Oskin's contorted face suggested he was feeling considerable pain. His companions mounted and escorted Oskin towards the outlet of Ghost Canyon, which was now clear of horses. They had no notion, however, of what the situation in the heart of the canyon was or of the whereabouts of Sturgis and his men, who might prove dangerous when they entered. Nor had they any knowledge of what had happened to Scott and Ruiz.

They rode cautiously with freshly loaded weapons, and travelled some distance along the now much trampled floor of the canyon without seeing signs of life. Rounding a twist in the steep walls, they came within sight of the high pueblo and the herd of W-Bar-F horses, calm now and moving towards the creek, attracted by the scent of water. Behind them, on foot, urging the animals along without spooking them, were Harry Scott and Pedro Ruiz.

'We'll move 'em on back home,' called Will Flinders. The horsemen placed themselves at points alongside the herd and assisted Scott and Ruiz in driving the animals along, with Oskin riding cautiously, obviously in some pain.

On the passage through the canyon, they saw the huddled bodies of four of the Peace Commission riders, victims of the sniping of Scott and Ruiz, but there was no sign of the live members of the Sturgis faction.

Unhurried progress brought them to the opening of the canyon, and the camp site of Scott and Ruiz, where they found the pair's horses still picketed. With Scott and Ruiz in their saddles, the party was able to move with more ease, although the recent exertions of the herd and the riders' mounts had wearied them to the extent that they could not achieve a brisk pace.

Out in the open land, they saw nothing of Sturgis and his remaining companions. They surmised that they had swallowed defeat and headed back to Vinegar Peak, but the W-Bar-F men kept up their watchfulness, since there were plenty of locations from where their opponents might spring an ambush.

They reached the W-Bar-F just after noon without any incident and immediately set about sorting the herd, segregating mares and stallions, placing some animals in the newly refurbished corrals and turning others out to pasture. Wrangling on saddle horses, already wearied, and work with a herd jaded by their strenuous experiences in the canyon, left the riders nearly exhausted and, after a supper at sundown, they turned in.

In the morning, Slim Oskin, who had contributed as best he could to the previous day's work, still complained of the pain in his ribs but stoically resisted the idea of seeking medical help. Dannehar told him he was a stubborn Yankee bullhead, and the rest of the crew settled the matter by informing Oskin that they would take him to Doc Furey in Vinegar Peak. His objections were not listened to.

144

An expedition by the full crew was settled on because of possible trouble with Sturgis and his crew when they reached town and Oskin would be taken in the buckboard to save him the strain of riding.

With Will Flinders driving the wagon and Oskin sprawled in it, the remainder formed outriders and the party entered the town at mid morning, keeping an alert vigilance for any sign of Sturgis and his men. They encountered an unexpected atmosphere.

Two or three of the people passing on the plankwalks waved greetings and it seemed that Vinegar Peak was displaying an unusually friendly disposition toward the Flinders brothers and their associates.

'What's got into this town?' asked Bert Flinders. 'I always said the place had the makings of a regular hole-in-the-wall outlaw town like Skeleton Flat. Now it's looking like the friendliest place on earth.'

They saw the blacksmith, Wally Drever, standing at the door of his forge. He nodded amiably, strode across the street and walked beside the buck-board.

'Are you fellows out to give Sturgis another shock?' he asked. 'You made him look damned helpless last time you were in town. Seems the folks here are giving you W-Bar-F men credit for giving

Bull Tuke and Billy Twist their come-uppance and causing the Peace Commission roughnecks to fall apart too. Vinegar Peak folk ain't worth much but there's a whole parcel of 'em plumb sorry for listening to all that gab from Sturgis and siding with him on his raid. There's been cases of folks reforming their behaviour fit to make a revival preacher green with envy. Darned if this ugly place isn't beginning to feel the glow of righteousness.'

One location to which feelings of righteousness did not extend was the upper floor of the Black Eagle building on the main street. There, Nate Sturgis and the remaining handful of his Peace Commission riders were crouched behind a window with their eyes on the newly arrived party.

The Peace Commission riders left four of their number dead in Ghost canyon. The five survivors had made a disgruntled retreat back to Vinegar Peak, on horses wearied by the bullet-dodgings and buffetings in the midst of the horse herd. Defeated in their objective of driving the W-Bar-F horses to destruction in the arroyo by the cunning sniping of Scott and Ruiz from the pueblo, they were now licking their wounds. While his hirelings were concealing their resentment at gaining nothing from being in the teeth of dire danger, Nate Sturgis was seething with renewed fanatical hatred of Dannehar, Oskin and the W-Bar-F crew.

Vicious little Shorty Sleeman, who had replaced

Bull Tuke as ramrod of the riders, gazed down at the passing buck-board and its passenger in the street and gave a grunt of satisfaction.

'We can shoot the whole boilin' of 'em from here,' he stated. 'We can get the whole bunch before they know what hit 'em.'

'No!' snapped Sturgis. 'I want them to know who hit them. This time, we'll get them for sure. It'll be sudden death, but they'll die knowing it was Nate Sturgis who dealt it out. Where are they headed?'

'Looks like they're going to Doc Furey's office across the street,' Sleeman said.

'Seems they have an injured man in the wagon,' said one of the riders. 'By grab, it's one of the gun-slingers, the skinniest one.'

'Not that he was injured by any of you *hombres*,' snorted Sturgis. 'You did hardly a damned thing back yonder in Ghost Canyon.'

'Hell, Mr Sturgis, that pair up on the canyon side had us flat footed with their sniping,' objected another rider.

'But you'll sure earn your corn now. We're going to leave that bunch stone cold. And we'll do it my way with everything properly planned,' stipulated Sturgis, with a determined glitter in his eyes. 'Get your weapons ready and do exactly as I tell you.'

CHAPTER TWELVE

BULLET-BITTEN SHOWDOWN

Out on the street, the W-Bar-F party halted at the boardwalk outside Doc Furey's office, dismounted and helped Slim Oskin out of the buck-board. Walking with some difficulty, he was assisted to the office by his companions and Bert Flinders hammered on the door vigorously.

It was opened by peppery Doc Furey, a whipcord-thin man with a large moustache. He was dressed in a crumpled black broadcloth suit, had a shellbelt about his middle and wore his customary touchy, tempered expression.

'Well? What do you want now that you've all but busted a man's door in?' he demanded.

148

'Got a patient for you, Doc. A man with something wrong with his ribs after a fall. Could be they're broken,' Bert Flinders said.

'Well, bring him in,' growled the doctor. 'Don't stand there giving me the benefit of your unqualified opinion. I'll decide whether he has broken ribs or not.'

Doc Furey was a Texan, an eccentric and something of an enigma. He was a Confederate veteran who had served as a wartime surgeon. In his civilian capacity, he was not a man to take sides. All Vinegar Peak knew, he was decidedly his own man. He might treat those associated with the Black Eagle outfit but he was no company man, nor was he a supporter of the supposed guardian of the town's wellbeing, the Peace Commission. He cared nothing for anyone's background or status. If they needed treatment, he treated them.

One hangover from his hectic days on the battlefield was the old pattern .44 Walker Colt, the favourite weapon of the first Texas Rangers, always holstered at his right hip. An oft-told popular yarn had it that, if Doc Furey failed to find a cure, he shot the patient – but he'd never been known to do so.

Oskin was taken into the office where there was a long wooden table to which Doc Furey nodded.

'Lay him out there and get his shirt off,' he ordered.

Oskin was laid on his back and, when he was shirtless and with his gunbelt removed, the doctor swabbed away the blood around his ribs and felt the area thoroughly, with Oskin uttering periodic growls and grunts.

'Quit complaining,' rumbled the doctor testily. 'I've taken arms and legs off men who made less fuss about it.' At length, he announced: 'He's got some deep cuts and abrasions but there's no sign of broken ribs. I reckon they're just bruised. I'll dress the cuts and strap up the ribs.'

The doctor collected materials and went to work on Oskin, strapping his ribs to the accompaniment of more grunts and much wriggling from the patient, to which the medical man paid not the slightest attention.

As he worked, Doc Furey commented with a chuckle: 'You fellows sure lit a fire under this blamed fool town when you dumped that gun-slinging pair on Sturgis. You went up in a lot of estimations, too. After all, they *were* Foxton and Brant not just any cheap gunnies. I don't know if you two strangers are just a pair of trail pilgrims or the hired gunnies folk think you are but I reckon your antics have brought about some changes. More than half of Vinegar Peak rode against the W-Bar-F a few nights back and now the same gallant souls are ready to cheer you fellows.'

'We noticed that,' replied Will Flinders. 'We

expected trouble when we showed up, but it seems almost everybody, even the stray dogs, were welcoming.'

'Because Sturgis has reigned too long as king of the heap,' the doctor said. 'He mesmerised folk into following him almost all the way to hell and led some to deaths and injury. Now, they're plumb ashamed of themselves for putting themselves in the hands of Sturgis and his roughnecks. What's more, it looks like Sturgis has come to the end of his rope. There's a strong rumour around the mine that the big men at the head office aim to fire him as president now that they know how he's been running things here.'

At that very moment, that same rumour was weighing heavily on the mind of Nate Sturgis as he looked out from the window across the street from the doctor's office. He had heard nothing official from the Kansas City headquarters, but disturbing whispered intelligence had filtered through to personnel at the mine, then to Sturgis. It held that the visiting directors who had witnessed the dumping of Foxton and Brant at his feet a few short hours before had been so profoundly unimpressed by his character and behaviour that Black Eagle's whole governing body had voted to eject him from his august office.

True or not, the rumour worked on his inflamed and warlike mood and fed his seething hatred of the Flinders brothers and the two supposed hired gunsharps who had hooked up with their crew. From the failed raid on the W-Bar-F and the dispatching of Bull Tuke and Billy Twist, to the last débâcle in Ghost Canyon, those two had been instrumental in forcefully pushing events his enemies' way. But, he vowed, the account was about to be settled in his favour.

He eyed Doc Furey's office with a savage gleam in his eyes. The whole W-Bar-F crew and those two skinny troublemakers were right there, almost in his hands. There was one way into the doctor's office, no back exit and a single window looking on to the street. His tactics on wider fields had failed but, right here in Vinegar Peak, he could deploy his forces effectively and achieve the vengeance he craved. His enemies could be bottled up in the small office and killing them was going to be like shooting fish in a barrel.

'Now listen,' he said, 'We'll work to a plan. The whole set of them are in that office and all armed. We move fast. Sleeman, only you and me will go in and concentrate on the gunslingers, while the rest of you cover the room from the window. I'll have a piece to say but not much, then we get to shooting without delay. Between us, we'll finish the whole lot before they get over their surprise. Leave Doc Furey alone unless he starts shooting with that Walker Colt of his, and he might well do.'

The street sweltered under the sun and tumble-weeds rolled lazily along it, driven by a slight breeze. Leaning on the jamb of the door of his forge, Wally Drever seemed to be dozing as the five surviving Peace Commission riders, led by Nate Sturgis, left the Black Eagle headquarters. All carried naked firearms and, soft footed as hunting Indians, they hastened across the street to Doc Furey's office.

There, Sturgis grabbed the door handle, twisted it quickly and thrust himself into the office speedily. By prior agreement, because of the cramped space in the office, only Shorty Sleeman, with a ready Colt, came behind him and slammed the door. Both he and Sturgis flattened their backs against it.

With his face contorted in furious anger, Sturgis glowered at the W-Bar-F men and the doctor – all of whom had turned to confront him on his sudden intrusion.

Before they had fully absorbed the situation, the men in the cramped room heard the crash of broken glass. A pane of the window was knocked in by a six-gun used as a hammer and the faces of the five Peace Commission toughs outside were seen peering in and flourishing weapons.

'Get the hell out of here!' roared Doc Furey, when he overcame the initial shock of the swift entry of Sturgis and Sleeman with their ready guns.

'Nothing doing, Doc,' responded Sturgis. 'I've got more than one bill to settle with this bunch and there's going to be a settlement pronto by the two of us here and the gents at the window. It's plumb gratifying to have the whole kit and kaboodle of the Flinders and their sidekicks all corked up in one bottle. It'll make things much easier.'

Sturgis grinned humourlessly as he levelled his gun, singling out Cephas Dannehar as his target. He was at the end of his rope, had been all but tumbled from his self appointed eminence as kingpin of Vinegar Peak and he knew it. But he had surprised the whole crew of his enemies, cornering them in boxed-in circumstances. Fish in a barrel, he thought to himself again with bloodthirsty satisfaction. And Dannehar would be the first to be dealt with.

Dannehar took Sturgis and Sleeman by surprise by abruptly dropping down to a squat, clawing for his holstered six-gun as he went, and clearing it from leather. Shorty Sleeman lunged forward, swinging the mouth of his gun downward, aiming point blank at Dannehar.

Dannehar fired when the short man was on the point of squeezing his trigger. The explosion of the gun was amplified by the restricted space of the office. A crimson splotch appeared on Sleeman's shirt in the region of his heart. His face suddenly went totally blank, his knees buckled and being close at hand in town.'

'And,' interjected the preacher, Levi Tibbins, 'they were so busy looking into the office that we just snuck up behind 'em and shoved our guns in their ribs before they could shoot at you fellows inside. They just dropped their guns right easy. There never was a better case of the Lord aiding the hands of the just.'

'What do you aim to do with us?' growled one of the scowling captives.

Drever gave a sharp laugh. 'Seems to me you can pack your sacks and go elsewhere, back to whatever drifting and devilment you were doing before you showed up here. We plan to form a citizens' committee and reform this place. It needs a genuine town council and someone better than Tom Cope as marshal. There'll be nothing for you to gain here.'

'Sure,' said Dannehar. 'Sturgis is dead and there'll be no more gun wages for you. Your best hope lies over the hill.'

'Unless you care to hang around until we decide to bring in United States marshals to look into the lawlessness that Sturgis stirred up,' grinned Drever. 'Who knows? Maybe some stretches in the penitentiary will result.'

'We'll ride,' stated the scowling man at once.

'Yeah. We'll ride,' affirmed a disgruntled companion. 'I was getting plumb sick of Sturgis, anyway. He took us into two disasters: one at the W-Bar-F and the other in Ghost Canyon.'

By this time, the rest of the W-Bar-F crew, with Doc Furey and Slim Oskin – shirtless and with his ribs strapped, had joined the tableau outside the doctor's office. A group of townsfolk had begun to cluster around the plankwalk, showing signs of satisfaction at the turn of events. Drever waved his hand towards them and told those held at gunpoint: 'All right, you'll be given an hour to pack and ride off yonder for good. I reckon there's enough men here who've recovered the civic dignity of Vinegar Peak to ride with you to the town limits and see you off the premises. Your day here is over. Go elsewhere and get in someone else's hair.'

Later, when the party from the W-Bar-F were preparing to leave town, Wally Drever joined them at their buck-board.

'What do you aim to do now?' asked Will Flinders.

'Make a move toward getting the town properly on its feet. Form a committee to steer the election of a regular town council and come to terms with the Black Eagle outfit, making it plain that the citizens run the town,' said Drever brightly. 'It might take a little time but you can already feel a fresh spirit in the place. It's the feel of eased consciences and folk recovering their dignity and independence.'

Back at the W-Bar-F, Dannehar and Oskin rested a couple of days to give Oskin's bruised ribs time to heal. In the course of their sojourn, Will Flinders said: 'You boys showed more than tolerable skill at wrangling cayuses. There's a couple of jobs here for you if you want them. We'll need more strength now that we've lost Bob Trickett.'

The pair shook their heads in unison. 'No,' said Dannehar. 'We appreciate the offer but we're both feeling the itch to ride and take a look over the next hill.'

In bright morning sunshine, the pair, provisioned for the trail, mounted up and said their farewells to the Flinders brothers and their crew.

They went northward and, half a day's wayfaring out of the Vinegar Peak country, they paused to eat beside a waterhole. Taking a brief rest afterwards, Oskin asked: 'Why do you figure everyone took us for gunslingers, anyhow? I figured we look like nothing but a pair of aimless trail tramps.'

Dannehar shrugged. 'I reckon we do, but I guess showing up to give Bert Flinders a hand when the Peace Commission gang nabbed him set off the notion that the Flinders boys had hired us. It was all a case of mistaken identity from the start.'

'Well, there's one sure thing,' said Oskin. 'As Bert Flinders pointed out, from here on in, we'll be tagged as the *hombres* who shot Foxton and Brant and that means there'll be plenty trying to stack up their reputations by gunning for us.'

Cephas Dannehar gave a crooked grin, stood up and strode for his horse. 'Sure,' he agreed. 'At least, the future won't be boring. C'mon, let's ride over that far horizon and discover who's going to shoot at us first.'